DEATH AT NEPTUNE YARD

A KIPPER COTTAGE MYSTERY

JAN DURHAM

INKUBATOR
BOOKS

Published by Inkubator Books
www.inkubatorbooks.com

ISBN (Paperback): 978-1-915275-18-9
ISBN (eBook): 978-1-915275-17-2
ISBN (Hardback) 978-1-915275-16-5

1

'What do you mean, you don't like the festival?' The Bride of Frankenstein glared at Detective Sergeant Kevin Ossett over his mug of tea.

Kevin shrugged. 'It's just all a bit daft, really, isn't it? Grown-up people messing around in fancy dress?'

His reaction surprised Liz McLuckie. Kevin was generally a fun-loving person in spite of his profession. If he didn't enjoy the annual Goth Festival, he was definitely in the minority. Most Whitby locals looked forward to it every year at Halloween, when the seaside town was invaded by hordes of pale-faced, black-eyed, steampunked Goths. It had been a tradition since the early nineties, inspired by the fact that Whitby Abbey ruins had featured in Bram Stoker's novel *Dracula*. In spite of its sinister origins, the festival was always fun, with music, cosplay and spookily themed events.

The Bride of Frankenstein, aka Liz's twenty-two-year-old archaeologist friend Niall Fitzgerald, who was currently staying in her cottage next door, pushed his mop of black hair out of his eyes to peer at his reflection in the mirror on the back of the cupboard door.

'I still think I look awesome,' he said.

'You do,' soothed Liz. 'Very awesome.' He was wearing a long, black Victorian dress, complete with corset and bustle. His face was bone-white, a jarring contrast with his blue eyes and the bloody gash across his throat. The gashes and stitches in his face and wrists looked all too realistic for Liz's liking – being an ex-accident and emergency nurse, she knew what she was talking about. Niall tweaked his veil and looked critically at the hem of his skirt, where it trailed over his Doc Martens boots.

'I'm not sure about the length, though. I might trip over it while I'm playing footie.' He eyed her sewing machine on the table. 'I don't suppose...'

She took the hint. 'Give it to me when you take it off. I'll lift it about an inch or so?'

'You're a star! I'd better get this lot off before I put the shower screen up next door.' He gulped down the rest of his tea and stomped up the narrow, wooden stairs.

Privately, Liz thought it was Niall who was the star. They'd befriended each other at the start of the summer, after he'd been fired from his archaeological dig at the abbey and they'd both been caught up in a sensational murder investigation that had almost ended in tragedy. Afterwards, she'd helped him find a place on a dig in Athens. He'd recently arrived back to help her get the cottage next door – Kipper Cottage – ready for its very first guests.

Liz had bought two adjoining eighteenth-century cottages – Kipper Cottage and Gull Cottage – the year before. She'd taken early retirement from her job in Edinburgh after the death of her husband, Mark. It was her intention to renovate both cottages, living in one and renting the other out as holiday accommodation. It had taken her almost five months to get Kipper ready, a real labour of love, and with less than a week to go before her guests arrived for the festival, she still had lots of odd jobs to finish off. The bathroom needed its shower screen and the rest of its fittings, the wall tiles were still to grout, and she still had curtains to make for the living room. Unfortunately, she kept getting sidetracked by costume-related favours for her friends. Which reminded her...

She turned to Kevin, who was trying to fish an unsuccessfully dunked biscuit from his tea with a finger.

'I don't suppose you could drop something at the café for me on your way back to work?' she asked.

He pulled a face. 'I'm not on foot.'

Liz's eyes widened. 'You mean you've had a squad car sitting outside my door all this time?' It was the sort of thing her neighbours in Henrietta Street would notice. Everyone made a point of knowing everyone else's business in Whitby. It irritated Liz sometimes, but was outweighed by the many, many benefits of living there.

'Sorry.' Kevin licked soggy biscuit off his finger and drained his mug. 'I'd better make tracks, or Flint will be wondering where I've got to.' Kevin's boss had transferred from the gritty streets of Middlesbrough in the spring and was still finding it hard to adjust to life in Whitby. It wasn't so much that the pace was slower, just... less predictable. Flexible wasn't really a word that could be used to describe Detective Inspector Flint.

'I can drop you in Church Street if you like?' said Kevin.

Liz shook her head. 'We could probably do with a leg stretch, couldn't we, Nelson?'

Hearing his name, Nelson the English bull terrier looked up from his basket and wagged his stumpy tail. He looked piratical, with his huge, coffin-shaped head and patch over one eye. Liz had heard certain unkind people call him the ugliest dog in Yorkshire. She didn't know about that, but after his heroic actions in the summer, she certainly knew he was the bravest.

She tidied the mugs off the table and put them in the sink.

'Niall, I'm going out!' she yelled up the stairs. 'Shouldn't be long.'

She grabbed her coat and the tote bag she had ready by the door, clipped Nelson onto his lead and followed Kevin out onto the narrow, cobbled street.

Outside, the air smelled of the sea. Herring gulls yodelled and swooped overhead, lifted on a breeze that ruffled their feathers. Kevin got into his car, waved to Liz and reversed back up the street. There was nowhere for him to turn around, because Henrietta Street ended, quite literally, in the sea. A landslide several years before had swept the cottages at the end of the terrace into the water, and the cliff above was still unstable. It was probably only a matter of time before all the cottages ended up in the sea, but that didn't bother her. She'd be long gone by then.

After Kevin's squad car had disappeared, Nelson pulled her along the old, cobbled street, between the two rows of pastel-painted cottages. It was a picture-perfect scene, complete with higgledy-piggledy roofs and Victorian street lamps. At the end of the street, they came to the bottom of the abbey steps, the one hundred and ninety-nine steps that led up the steep slope to St Mary's Church and the ruined medieval abbey. The abbey had first been a Christian monastery, then a Benedictine abbey, one of the key centres of learning and culture in Northern Europe. The steps that led up to it had been worn smooth over the centuries by the feet of pilgrims, tourists and sensation-seekers, eager to see the ruins that inspired Bram Stoker's *Dracula*.

Nelson huffed as she pulled him past the bottom of the steps, clearly disappointed not to be going up them – St

Mary's graveyard on the clifftop was his favourite place in the world. He seemed quite resigned to his fate, however, until they went a few more metres, and Liz tried to lead him past the wrought-iron gate that led to Neptune Yard, a small enclave of cottages accessed by a narrow alleyway. He came to an abrupt halt. His hackles went up. He stared, unblinking, into the alley beyond the gate.

'What's the matter?' She peered down the alley. It was dark, and she couldn't see what had upset him. She supposed it must be a cat, even though he usually ignored them. 'Come on, let's go.' He lifted his nose, sniffed the air, and growled, low in his throat. Not like him at all. She tugged on the lead, but still he didn't budge. Eventually she had to use all her strength to haul him away from the gate, into Church Street.

'Whatever's got into you?' she asked. Nelson just gave her an enigmatic look and trotted on.

Whitby, on the North Yorkshire coast, was a town of two halves. Liz lived on the East Cliff, in the oldest part, that had mostly been built in the eighteen hundreds. It was packed with fishermen's cottages, a couple of coaching inns and many small independent shops selling souvenirs, ice cream, and the famous Whitby Jet jewellery. It was dominated by the abbey and St Mary's Church, both attracting visitors from all over the world.

The West Cliff, on the other side of the harbour, was more modern – a typical Victorian seaside resort, with a pier, pastel-painted hotels, amusement arcades, contemporary shops and, of course, the main beach – ever popular with families. The two parts were linked by a bridge that swung open to allow boats to pass from the fishing harbour into the marina. Today, however, Liz's destination was the Full Moon café, owned by her friends Tilly and Mags, which meant she didn't need to cross the water.

Church Street was busy, but nowhere near as crowded as

it had been at the height of the summer; it only took Liz five minutes to reach the Dickensian-windowed café on Sandgate. The window displays had been prepared for the festival, decorated with all things spooky – spell books, potions, cobwebs and pumpkins. In pride of place was Tilly's prize possession, her Hand of Glory, a grisly mummified hand said to bestow the gift of supernatural stealth on any burglar who carried it. As far as Liz knew, Tilly hadn't put it to the test yet. If her wife, Mags, had anything to do with it, she never would.

The moment Liz stepped inside the café, she could tell there was something wrong. The interior was the same as ever, bookshelves and comfy leather chairs at one end, and café tables at the other, decorated in a hotchpotch of antiques and found treasures. But Tilly, with her white-blonde cropped hair, wearing a pair of neon-pink dungarees, was huddled over the counter with Grazyna, her Polish assistant manager, a statuesque brunette who always looked as if she was about to punch someone. They both looked up as Liz came in. Neither was smiling. That wasn't surprising for Grazyna, but was unusual for Tilly.

'What's up?' she asked, unclipping Nelson from his lead. He made a beeline for his usual spot behind the counter and found the rubber pig Tilly kept there for him.

'Iris is in hospital,' said Tilly.

'What?' Iris Gladwell was a café regular, who did changeover cleaning for many of the holiday cottages in the town. Liz guessed she was somewhere in her seventies. She had the air of a bustling sergeant major and a booming voice to match. 'What's wrong with her?'

'Suspected heart attack. She was rushed in last night.'

'That's awful.' Liz could hardly believe it. She'd always thought of Iris as indestructible. 'Has anyone been to see her yet?'

'Not yet,' said Tilly.

'I would visit her,' said Grazyna, 'but Lukasz and Eryk have dental appointments this afternoon. It has taken me many weeks to persuade them, and they only agreed to go if I promised to take them to the cinema afterwards.'

'And we have an eighteenth birthday party to cater for tonight,' said Tilly. 'But I suppose we *could* cancel.'

'Don't be daft,' said Liz. 'You can't ruin someone's birthday. I'll go. Where've they taken her?'

'The community hospital,' said Tilly. 'But her son, Irwin, says they might transfer her to Middlesbrough.'

Liz didn't know Iris had a son. Somehow she'd imagined her as a lone force of nature, born of Yorkshire grit and hard weather.

Grazyna went to take the order of an elderly couple at one of the tables.

'Before I forget,' said Liz to Tilly, 'here's your cape.' She handed her the tote bag.

'Oh!' Tilly clapped her hands. 'Can I try it on?' She didn't wait for an answer, pulling it out of the bag and wrapping herself in the red velvet fabric. She examined her reflection in the window. 'It's gorgeous. Thank you.'

'You're welcome.'

'How're things going with Kipper Cottage?' asked Tilly.

'Not too bad. I just have the bathroom fittings to put up and curtains to make. Oh... and the grouting in the shower.'

'Cool!'

It was. It had been the culmination of a lot of hard work getting to this point, but as the day of her guests' arrival came closer, Liz was feeling more than a little nervous. What if they didn't like the cottage?

She realised Tilly was watching her.

'Relax,' Tilly said. 'They'll love it.'

Liz nodded and changed the subject. 'How's your licence

application coming on?' Tilly had applied to the council for a temporary drinks licence so she could serve alcohol during the festival.

Tilly looked glum. 'I haven't heard anything yet. They're cutting it really fine. If I don't hear in the next couple of days, I won't have time to buy stock.'

'They probably have a backlog,' suggested Liz.

'Probably.' Tilly sighed. 'I've been stressed about it, but poor Iris put my worries into perspective. I hope she's going to be okay.'

Liz hoped so too.

'I'll make up a goodie bag for you to take to her,' said Tilly. 'I'm not sure what visiting hours are, though.'

'I'll call the hospital first,' said Liz. 'To see if she's well enough for visitors, and make sure she hasn't been transferred to Middlesbrough.'

SHE NEEDN'T HAVE WORRIED on either score. Later that afternoon, she found Iris in the hospital, sitting up in bed, dressed in a tartan bed jacket, looking remarkably perky for someone who'd had a close brush with death. Iris didn't spot Liz at first – she was too busy berating the young nurse who was trying to take her temperature.

'CAN'T YOU UNHOOK ME FROM THIS MACHINE?' she bellowed around the thermometer. 'I CAN'T BLOODY MOVE!'

'You know I can't do that, Mrs Gladwell. We need to keep an eye on you.'

'WHAT IF I NEED A WEE?'

'Ring the buzzer, and we'll come and help you.'

Iris glared at the bedpan. 'I'M NOT WEEING IN THAT AGAIN. IF YOU THINK I AM, YOU CAN BLOODY WELL THINK AGAIN.'

There were two other beds on the ward. The occupants –
a middle-aged man and an elderly woman – looked a little
dazed, which wasn't surprising. Iris was unable to speak at
any volume below a bellow. When Liz had first met her, she
supposed it was because the old lady was deaf. But apparently not. Apparently she'd shouted like that all her life.

The old lady spotted her. 'LIZ! THANK GOD! PLEASE
TELL ME YOU'VE BROUGHT SOMETHING TO EAT. THE
FOOD IN HERE IS AWFUL.'

The nurse made a note on Iris's chart and met Liz's eye as
she headed out. Her look said everything she wasn't
permitted to say aloud. Liz suppressed a grin and joined Iris
at the bed.

'I've brought you some of Tilly's scones and jam if you
want it.'

'WHAT DAY IS IT?'

'Monday.'

'YOU KNOW I CAN'T EAT JAM ON A MONDAY,' she
bellowed, 'BUT I'LL HAVE THE SCONES.'

Liz grinned. She'd forgotten that Iris had very specific and
unfathomable rules about eating jam. 'How are you? You look
a lot better than I expected you to.'

'THERE'S NOTHING WRONG WITH ME.'

'Which is why you're in here, I suppose?' said Liz, with
irony.

Iris harrumphed. 'THEY'VE MADE SOMETHING OUT
OF NOTHING. MY HEART'S FINE. I GOT A SHOCK, IS
ALL.'

'A shock?'

'YOU'D HAVE HAD A SHOCK TOO IF YOU'D
SEEN IT.'

Liz frowned. 'Seen what?'

Iris grabbed Liz's wrist. 'THE BARGHEST! THE DOG OF
DEATH!'

2

L iz gently disengaged her wrist from Iris's iron grip.

'What?'

'THE BARGHEST!'

Liz glanced at the heart monitor. It was beeping quite fast.

'SOMEONE'S GOING TO DIE!'

Liz thought it was likely to be Iris if she didn't calm down.

'I'm sorry,' she said. 'You've lost me.'

'It's an old Whitby legend.' Liz turned at a new voice. A short man of about forty wearing glasses and a lilac jumper put two takeaway coffee cups on Iris's locker. 'A big black dog. Whenever it's seen in the town, someone dies.'

'AND I DIDN'T!' yelled Iris triumphantly.

'Don't speak too soon,' the man said. 'There's still time for one of the nurses to do you in.' He pushed his glasses further up his nose and held out his hand to Liz.

'Irwin Gladwell.'

'I'm Liz. Iris's friend.'

Irwin raised an eyebrow.

'I DO HAVE FRIENDS, YOU KNOW,' yelled Iris.

'Miraculously.'

Iris ignored the barb and fixed Liz with her watery blue stare. 'I SAW THE BARGHEST THROUGH THE WINDOW. A GREAT, BLACK, SHAGGY BEAST. JUST STANDING THERE IN THE YARD. IT LOOKED STRAIGHT AT ME, AND EVERYTHING WENT COLD.'

Liz met her gaze. It didn't waver. The old lady was convinced she was telling the truth. But what she *thought* she saw and what she *actually* saw could be two different things.

'Donnie Satterthwaite's outside,' said Irwin to Iris. 'He wants to talk to you.'

Iris's eyes opened wide. Satterthwaite was a journalist for the *Whitby Bugle*, admired and despised in equal measure, depending on which side of his current story you stood.

'He's heard about your brush with supernatural forces. I can't imagine how, when you've kept it such a secret.' Irwin delivered the line deadpan.

'HE THINKS HE'S FUNNY,' Iris shouted to Liz. She turned back to Irwin. 'WELL, DON'T JUST HANG ABOUT, SHOW HIM IN!'

'I'll get him,' said Liz. 'I'll leave you to it.' She leaned over and kissed Iris's cheek. 'I'll be back tomorrow. Enjoy your scones.'

She was relieved to have an excuse to go. She really didn't like hospitals, which was surprising considering she'd spent most of her working life in them. Perhaps it was because she'd spent too many hours on the other side of the fence, when Mark had been ill?

She headed out into the corridor. Donnie Satterthwaite was waiting on one of the plastic chairs. Liz recognised him from his byline photo in the *Bugle*. He was a tall man, with a shock of ginger hair and a shrewd expression.

'You can go in,' said Liz. She hesitated and then decided to speak. 'I hope you're not going to make her look silly.'

'Why would I do that?' said Satterthwaite. 'I believe her, one hundred per cent.'

'You do?'

Satterthwaite nodded. 'I live in Neptune Yard too, and I heard the dog. So did one of our neighbours.'

'What did it sound like?'

'Horrible. I'd never really understood the phrase "made my blood run cold" before, but that's exactly what it did.' There wasn't a trace of irony or scepticism on the journalist's face. 'I can't wait to hear what it looked like.'

'ARE YOU OUT THERE, DONALD?' Iris's voice boomed from inside the ward. 'STOP FANNYING ABOUT AND COME ON IN.'

'OH MY GOD!' Tilly clapped her hands. 'Iris is famous! Read it out to us, B!'

They were sitting at the scrubbed pine table in the kitchen of Liz's friend Benedict. The room was big but cosy, with chunky cabinets, a butler's sink, and a huge blue Aga. There were several cats draped on the furniture and windowsills – a legacy from Benedict's wife, Katherine, who had died the previous year. Benedict had invited Liz, Tilly and Niall for supper, but they'd been distracted from the food by Kevin's late arrival with the evening newspaper. Benedict read it aloud.

'Mysterious sighting of demon dog leads to hospitalisation of OAP.'

'Awful clunky headline,' sniffed Niall.

Benedict read on. *'Something big, black and distinctly doglike is prowling the streets of Whitby. Police are taking the sighting seriously, but admit they are baffled.'*

'That's bollocks,' said Kevin. 'As far as I know, no one has reported anything.'

Benedict ran a hand through his hair. The flashes of white in it were the only thing that betrayed his fifty-something years; otherwise he was lean and athletic, almost boyish looking.

'Are you going to let me read this or not?' he asked Kevin.

Kevin nodded.

Benedict read on. *'The purported beast, Whitby's answer to Bigfoot and the Loch Ness monster, has been a major topic of conversation in the town ever since it was seen by Mrs Iris Gladwell in Neptune Yard yesterday evening. It frightened her so much that she had a cardiac arrest and had to be rushed to the Whitby community hospital. Some people might dismiss the sighting as an old woman's imagination...'*

'Jaysus,' muttered Niall, 'she won't like that.'

'The doctors say it was a cardiac "event" anyway, not an arrest,' said Liz. 'But I'm not really sure what that means.'

'Shh!' hissed Tilly. 'For heaven's sake, let B finish.'

'... if it wasn't for the fact that the sighting was preceded by eerie howling, heard by three of Mrs Gladwell's neighbours, including this journalist and Mr Gordon Parker of Starfish Cottage, who described the noise as "the uncanniest thing I've ever heard." Mrs Gladwell also described her encounter with the beast. "I couldn't believe my eyes," she said. "It was as big as a calf, if not bigger, and had huge, staring eyes. I don't dare go out in my yard now."'

Niall sniggered. 'That must be the quietest Iris has ever said anything.'

Benedict continued, *'These uncanny events have preceded the annual arrival of Goths in the town...'* He stopped and scanned the rest. 'He goes on a bit more about the festival, but that's about it.'

'So her neighbours heard it?' said Tilly. 'That's scary.'

It was. Liz had forgotten Iris lived in Neptune Yard. She remembered Nelson's strange behaviour at the gate that morning. Had it been a coincidence?

Kevin helped himself to a bowl of goulash from the pot on the table and plonked himself down.

'This looks great, Dad.' He sniffed the contents. 'Smells great too. Is there any bread?'

'I'll cut you some more.' Benedict got up. Liz tried not to watch him as he went to the kitchen counter. She liked the way he moved.

'What, exactly, is the Barghest?' she asked Tilly.

Tilly leaned forward, her own meal forgotten. 'An old Whitby legend. A big, black dog haunts the town just before someone dies. Locals use it to scare their kids into behaving.'

'Perhaps Grazyna should try it on Lukasz and Eryk,' suggested Liz. The boys had only been in the town a few months, but were already notorious.

'It isn't just an old wives' tale,' said Niall. 'When the Roman signalling station at Goldsborough was excavated, they found a grave. A man and a massive dog. They'd died fighting each other.'

Tilly scoffed. 'You're having us on.'

'I am not!'

'It's true.' Benedict put more bread in the middle of the table. 'The dog had its teeth in the man's throat. The excavation was sometime in the early nineteen hundreds, wasn't it?'

'Yeah.' Niall nodded. 'Hornsby and Laverick.'

'I wish Mags was here,' said Tilly. 'She loves this kind of stuff. Anything spooky or witchy.'

'Where is she, anyway?' asked Niall.

'Gone to the movies with Grazyna and the boys.'

Liz looked at Benedict. 'I thought Gillian would be here too.'

'She has a confirmation class. But sends her love.'

Reverend Gillian Garraway and Benedict had been an item since the summer. The start of their romance had coincided, unfortunately, with Liz's realisation that what she felt for Benedict was more than friendship. It had come as a huge surprise to her. Ever since Mark's death five years before, she'd convinced herself that part of her life – the romantic part – was over. But apparently it wasn't. She'd found it hard to watch Benedict and Gillian's blossoming relationship, but just had to keep reminding herself that jealousy was an ugly emotion, particularly for a woman in her fifties who should know better.

'More goulash, Liz?' asked Benedict.

She smiled. 'Please. It's delicious.'

They were interrupted by a buzzing noise. After a few moments of stunned silence, they realised it was coming from the pocket of Kevin's jacket on the back of his chair. Kevin kept eating.

'Shouldn't you answer that?' asked Tilly.

'It'll just be Flint wanting to know why I haven't filed some report or other.'

The phone continued to buzz. Kevin continued to ignore it. Whoever it was kept redialling rather than leave a message.

'It might be important,' said Tilly.

Kevin sighed and rummaged in his pocket. He pulled out his phone to answer it.

'Ossett... yes... sorry... I was having dinner.' As he listened to the voice on the other end, his face grew more and more serious. 'I'll be there in half an hour... Okay, okay... fifteen minutes, then.' He hung up.

'I told you it might be serious,' said Tilly. 'What is it?'

'You're never going to believe this,' said Kevin. 'Donnie Satterthwaite's dead.'

3

The walls in Kipper Cottage were all out of whack. Made from eighteenth-century horsehair and plaster, they bulged and dipped in unexpected places, which had made tiling the bathroom something of a challenge. In the end Liz had had to resort to relining the shower enclosure with new plasterboard, an expense she hadn't anticipated. Luckily, she'd found some lovely Delft-style blue and white tiles in the bargain bin of the DIY superstore in Scarborough. There had been exactly the right number of tiles, which was great, but it meant she couldn't afford to lose any due to careless cutting or accidental breakage. Liz had managed not to waste any, although she suspected it had been more through luck than skill.

Now the tiles were on, she was very pleased with the effect. All she had to do was finish the grouting. It was one of her least favourite jobs. She hated the feel of the grout as it dried on her hands, and no matter how careful she was, she still managed to get most of it on the tiles themselves, which made clean-up difficult.

The left-hand side of the enclosure was done, and she

was just about to start on the back when someone knocked at the door downstairs.

Yip, yip, yip!

Nelson signalled the visitor with his usual bark.

'Damn.' Liz cleaned her hands the best she could on her overalls and went downstairs to answer it.

It was Kevin.

'Can I have a cuppa?' he asked. His scrubbed schoolboy face was unusually pale.

'Of course,' said Liz. 'Are you okay?'

'Not really.'

She ushered him in. 'Put the kettle on,' she said. 'I'll just nip upstairs to put the lid on my grout.'

She washed her hands while she was up there, and when she came down, she found Kevin sitting at the kitchen table, staring into space. She filled the kettle and put it on.

'Sorry,' said Kevin. 'You asked me to do that. You're busy. I don't want to bother you.'

'Don't be daft. What's happened?'

'I've been in Neptune Yard and really needed a breather.'

'So it's a crime scene?' She'd thought Donnie Satterthwaite might have had a fatal accident or even had a heart attack like Iris. Although two heart attacks in Neptune Yard within a couple of days was a bit of a coincidence.

'It was horrible,' muttered Kevin. 'His eyes were open, and he had the most terrible look on his face. I don't care if I never see anything like it again.'

Liz could sympathise. Death was always shocking, even when it came peacefully. But what Kevin said next surprised her.

'He heard the Barghest too.'

She frowned. Satterthwaite had told her the sound had made his blood run cold. 'What's that got to do with it?' She looked at Kevin, hard. She knew him well enough to know there was something he wasn't telling her. 'Well?' she prompted.

He hesitated. 'He looked like he'd been scared to death. And... there was a bloody great paw print on the wall.'

'What?'

'As big as a dinner plate. On the kitchen wall. We still have to test what the mark is made of, but it looks like blood.'

They stared at each other a long moment.

'It's not the Barghest,' said Liz, at last.

'How do you know?'

'Because ghosts and demons don't exist,' she said. 'And dogs don't walk on walls.'

Someone knocked at the door.

Yip, yip, yip!

Nelson gave immediate lie to what she'd just said by leaping up at the door and putting his paws on it. Kevin threw Liz a triumphant look, which she ignored, as she grabbed Nelson's collar and opened the door. A woman glared at her from the step. She was wearing a trouser suit and trainers, and her hair was cut into an immaculate chin-length bob.

'Detective Inspector Flint,' said Liz wearily.

'He's here, I suppose?' Flint's eyes were as hard as pebbles.

Liz didn't have to ask who 'he' was. She wrestled Nelson away from the door and opened it wider for the detective to march inside.

'I thought I'd find you here,' she snapped at Kevin. 'You're supposed to be at the cr—' She broke off and glanced at Liz. 'At the cottage.'

'I'm due a break,' said Kevin.

'You take one when I say so.' She narrowed her eyes at him. 'I hope you haven't been blabbing to Mrs McLuckie.'

'Of course he hasn't! ' Liz avoided Kevin's eye as she said

it. 'He just came in for a cup of tea. I take it you don't want one?'

'You don't have time for that,' said Flint to Kevin. 'We need to get to the *Bugle*, pronto.'

'Why?' he asked.

'We have to put a lid on things. Make sure no one gets hold of this story and blows it out of proportion.'

'Oh,' said Liz, wide-eyed, 'has something happened?'

Flint didn't bother to answer, but marched out. Kevin followed, with an apologetic look at Liz. Liz closed the door behind them and caught Nelson's eye.

'She *is* a bit rude. Don't take it personally. I don't think she can help it.'

Nelson looked sceptical.

Liz sighed. She really didn't feel like going back to her grouting. Perhaps it was a good time to take a break? She caught Nelson's eye again and said his favourite word.

'Walk?'

THE VIEW from halfway up the abbey steps never failed to lift Liz's spirits. The old town of Whitby stretched out below her, a haphazard jumble of cottages and red-tiled roofs. Although the air was chilly, there was no breeze, and threads of smoke rose vertically from many of the chimneys. Just beyond the old town lay the harbour. Only a couple of fishing boats were currently moored in the smooth pewter-coloured water. Behind them, above the dockside pubs and amusement arcades, was the West Cliff, topped with rows of elegant pastel-coloured hotels and apartment blocks. To their right beyond the West Cliff pier seethed the dangerous waters of the North Sea.

Liz was standing on one of the coffin steps, so called because they'd been made deeper for funeral processions to rest on the way up to St Mary's graveyard. Unusually, there was no one else around. Liz knew it would change again in the next few days, when people started to arrive for the Goth Festival. For the moment, however, she enjoyed the sensation of having the whole town to herself, even if it was just an illusion. She took a deep breath of salty air. It was scented with woodsmoke from the smokery that stood beside her own cottages on Henrietta Street, where rows of herring hung from beams, cured by fires beneath, transforming into world-famous Whitby kippers. A solitary puff of wind stirred Liz's hair. She shivered and pulled her coat a little tighter. Winter was definitely on its way.

She set off again up the steps. Or rather, she tried to. Nelson wouldn't budge. He just sat there facing the sea, ears pricked, nose lifted.

'Come on,' she said. She tugged his lead, but still he refused to move. She didn't understand it. Ordinarily, he would be pulling her up the steps as fast as he could, eager to be up in St Mary's graveyard, where he could be off his lead.

'What's the matter? Don't you want to chase rabbits today?' She tried pulling him upwards, but he wouldn't budge. Nelson wasn't a big dog, but he was a bundle of muscle. It was like trying to shift a boulder.

'Rabbits, Nelson?'

He lifted his nose higher. And howled. A long, mournful wail that seemed to go on forever and made the hairs on the back of her neck stand on end. Then he snapped his jaws together and took off! Not *up* the steps, but *down* again, pulling her after him.

'Stop!' she gasped. 'Nelson!'

Her astonishment quickly turned to fear as they careered downwards. She couldn't keep up. If she wasn't careful, he'd break her neck. She had no choice but to let go of his lead.

The leather flew from her fingers, and she could only

watch, open-mouthed, as he cannonballed the rest of the way down the steps. Then he shot left, out of sight.

She couldn't believe what had happened. She'd never heard Nelson howl before, not once, ever since she'd adopted him from the animal shelter the year before. She hurried down the steps after him, terrified he might do himself or someone else an injury. When she got to the bottom, she was relieved to see he hadn't gone far, but had stopped at the entrance to Neptune Yard. His nose was thrust through the bars of the gate, and every hair on the back of his neck was standing to attention. Liz ran to him and grabbed his trailing lead.

'Bad boy! What on earth's the matter with you?' She peered down the alleyway, but it was dark, and she couldn't see anything out of the ordinary. As she looked, however, a strange sensation crept over her. Someone – or something – was watching them.

'That dog of yours is dangerous,' said a voice above them.

Nelson's head snapped up.

'He should be muzzled.'

It was Nelson's nemesis, Dora Spackle, curator of the abbey museum. Wisely, she had issued her proclamation from the safety of the steps – only her head was visible over the railing above them, adorned in her favourite twenties-style cloche hat.

Liz snapped, 'When I want your opinion, I'll ask for it.' She was in no mood for Dora's middle-aged sniping today. Neither was Nelson.

Yip, yip, yip!

Dora's head vanished from sight. Nelson allowed Liz to pull him away from the gate and past the bottom of the abbey steps.

Yip, yip!

He couldn't resist one last defiant bark at Dora's back as she hurried up the steps away from them.

Their feud had started the winter before, sparked by an incident involving Nelson's bladder, one of Dora's handbags, and a vindictive kick that had, thankfully, missed Nelson's ribs by less than a millimetre. Now Nelson tried to take a chunk out of Dora whenever he could. Liz didn't think he actually *would* bite her if it actually came to it, but he gave a very convincing impression of wanting to, and she preferred not to put it to the test. Today, as much as Liz was irritated by Dora and her ongoing vendetta with Nelson, she was glad she'd been there to distract him.

Liz walked up Henrietta Street, back to the cottages. Nelson trotted beside her on the cobbles, as if nothing had happened. Liz wasn't quite so sanguine. She couldn't shake off the unnerving sensation she'd had at the gate to Neptune Yard. She didn't think it had been her imagination.

Who – or what – had been watching them?

4

With only twenty-four hours to go before her guests arrived at Kipper Cottage, Liz had only just started to make the kitchen curtains. She spent the morning on her knees, cutting and measuring fabric, trying to avoid Niall, who was blundering around the kitchen in his boots, touching up patches on the ceiling with emulsion.

'If you get any paint on this material, I'll kill you.'

'Don't worry, Mrs Mac. I'm a professional.'

He wasn't, of course, but she had to admit he was a very handy amateur. He'd jumped at the chance to earn some money by helping Liz get Kipper ready for her guests. He was trying to save enough to go back to Dublin for Christmas, without alerting his mother to the fact he was struggling for money.

'My uncle Finn was a painter and decorator,' he said.

'Oh?' *Here we go*, thought Liz. Niall had many, many relatives, all with a tall tale attached.

Niall nodded. 'He used to help my da with some of his building projects. But then he went blind.' He leaned into the corner on his stool to reach a particularly tricky bit of ceiling. 'Turned out he'd been using some *really* dodgy paint. On the cheap. The fumes made him lose his sight.'

'That's awful,' said Liz, genuinely appalled.

'It didn't stop him from painting, though. As long as everything was all the same colour.' He caught Liz's eye. 'No cutting in.'

Liz looked at him.

'My aunt Clodagh was no oil painting, so we all thought it was a blessing him losing his sight anyway.'

Liz got it. 'You're pulling my leg.'

'Just a bit.' Niall grinned. 'You *are* quite easy to wind up, Mrs Mac.'

'As long as I keep you amused,' said Liz tartly. She gathered up all her pieces of cut fabric and took them to the table where her sewing machine was waiting. Niall clomped down off his stool and peered up at the ceiling.

'I think that'll do.'

She checked. 'Looks good to me.'

A sudden rumbling made Nelson lift his head from his basket. Niall looked sheepish.

'Is that your stomach?' asked Liz.

Niall nodded. 'I don't suppose it's lunchtime yet?'

LIZ WAS ALWAYS astonished by how much food Niall could tuck into his skinny frame. She watched him polish off a bowl of soup in the café, followed by lasagne and chips, and then fruit crumble and custard. Having only had a tuna toastie herself, Liz was already finished her lunch.

'Can I fill that up again for you?' asked Tilly, nodding at Liz's empty pot of tea.

'It's okay, thanks. I have to be getting back to my curtains.'

'Did you hear Iris is out of hospital?'

'That was quick.'

'Apparently it was just an angina attack. The doctor's keeping his eye on her, but reckons she'll be okay.'

'The woman has the constitution of an ox,' said Niall. 'She'll outlive all of us.'

Tilly disappeared back into the kitchen.

The café was busy, mostly with locals, and a couple of older tourists. One lone Goth, a young woman dressed entirely in black, sat at the library end of the café, reading a book and sipping coffee – a vanguard for the coming hordes. Grazyna was waiting tables, and Lukasz and Eryk were eating their lunch, dark heads bent over their food. They were ten years old – robust, energetic boys, always on the move, virtually identical to each other except that Eryk's hair was shorter and spikier.

'I wonder why they don't have lunch at school,' mused Liz to Niall.

'I think Grazyna likes to keep her eye on them,' he said around a mouthful of crumble.

'Very wise.' Liz watched them. They were quieter than usual. No banter or laughter as they ate their food. Instead they leaned in close, whispering to each other. If Liz had to use a word to describe them, it would be conspiratorial. It didn't bode well for Grazyna.

Tilly re-emerged from the kitchen, waving a brown envelope.

'Look what just arrived,' she said.

'News about your licence application?' asked Liz.

Tilly nodded.

'Open it, then,' urged Niall.

Tilly hesitated. Having a licence to serve alcohol during the festival could potentially make a huge difference to her income. She ripped open the envelope and read the contents.

From her dour expression, Liz and Niall could tell it wasn't good news.

'Oh, well.' Tilly crumpled the letter. 'It was worth a try.'

'Bloody council,' said Niall.

Tilly nodded. 'I'd better let Mags know.' She retreated to the kitchen.

Liz and Niall met each other's eye.

'Ouch,' said Niall in solidarity.

'Ouch is right. The festival only happens once a year; she needs to make the most of it.'

The bell above the door rang as it was opened, making the pair look up. Kevin entered and joined them at the table, but Liz's attention was caught by Eryk and Lukasz. They stared at Kevin, pushed their chairs back and clattered out of the café. They hadn't even finished their lunch.

'Was it something I said?' asked Kevin with a grin. He picked up the menu. 'What's today's special? I'm starving.'

'You're feeling better now, then?' asked Liz.

'Yes, sorry about that. I'm usually okay around corpses.'

'I take it we're talking about Donnie Satterthwaite?' said Niall, eyes bright with curiosity. 'What was so terrible about him?'

Liz saved Kevin from answering. 'He looked as if he'd been scared to death.'

'Turns out he wasn't,' said Kevin, matter-of-fact.

'Oh?' Liz met Niall's eye over the table.

'It was something else,' said Kevin.

There was a long pause while Kevin made a show of reading the menu.

'Come on, man, don't be a tease,' said Niall.

Kevin sighed. He knew when he was outnumbered. 'The toxicology report says he had strychnine in his system.'

'Strychnine?' echoed Niall.

'Very Agatha Christie,' said Liz.

'Keep that to yourselves, please. It isn't common knowledge.' Kevin looked around. There was no sign of Tilly or Grazyna. 'What does a man have to do to get food around here?'

LIZ THOUGHT about what Kevin had told them while she sewed header tape to her curtains. Strychnine was a very old-fashioned poison, readily available in pesticides during the Golden Age of crime writing, but not so much now. In truth, strychnine poisoning hadn't been common even then, but like its poisonous partner in crime, cyanide, it had been a handy solution for writers looking for a bloodless crime. Strychnine and cyanide were largely interchangeable in novels, but in real life, their effects were very different. Cyanide worked fast, with loss of consciousness and death coming quickly. Strychnine, on the other hand, produced some of the most extreme and painful symptoms of any toxic reaction – terrible muscle spasms and contortions of the body. Satterthwaite might have looked as if he'd been scared to death, but his death was likely due to either asphyxiation, caused by paralysis of the neural pathways that controlled breathing, or exhaustion from the spasms. He'd probably taken two to three hours to die, and had been conscious throughout.

Liz couldn't think of a worse way to go. She wondered who could have hated Satterthwaite that much. He must have fallen out with quite a few people over the years, thanks to the stinging articles he'd written in the *Bugle*. But even so... Liz shuddered. And, of course, there was the paw print. What, if anything, did it have to do with Satterthwaite's murder? He'd also heard the ghostly howling in Neptune Yard.

Iris's warning came back to her. *SOMEONE'S GOING TO DIE!*

Iris had been right, but Liz didn't believe in ghosts and ghouls. There had to be a rational explanation.

She finished sewing and cut the thread. The curtains were done. They needed ironing and hanging, but there would be enough time to do that in the morning, before her guests arrived. Liz shook them out and draped them over the back of her chair. Then she looked at her watch. Seven o'clock. It wasn't too late to pay a visit.

She popped into Gull Cottage next door to pick up some bits and pieces she'd bought, and found Niall there getting ready to go out.

'The Duke of York asked me to do a shift,' he said. 'They heard I was back in town.'

'That's great,' said Liz. 'They'll find the extra pair of hands useful during the festival.'

'And an extra quid or two in my pocket won't hurt, either.' Niall grinned.

He eyed the basket of fruit she was carrying. 'Are you off to see Iris? Hang on a minute, and I'll come with you.'

They walked down Henrietta Street together and parted company at the Duke of York, which faced the bottom of the abbey steps, only a few metres from the entrance to Neptune Yard.

Liz was apprehensive as she unlatched the gate and pushed it open, but, although the alleyway was dark, she didn't feel she was being watched like the last time. Iris's cottage – Benbow Cottage – was the first in the yard. There were half a dozen cottages in total, arranged in a higgledy-piggledy fashion, some side-on and some facing each other across the square. At the furthest end there was a small, fenced allotment. One of the cottage doors had yellow tape across it – Satterthwaite's and still officially a crime scene. Liz was filled with curiosity. She resisted the urge to cross the yard and peer through his window. She knocked on Iris's door instead.

It was a moment or two before Irwin answered, with flour on his hands. He wiped his hands on his old-fashioned pinny and ushered her inside.

'WHO IS IT?' Iris yelled. 'IS IT SOMEONE TO SEE ME? I'LL COME DOWN.'

'No, Mother!' Irwin called back up the stairs. 'Stay where you are!' He turned to Liz. 'I'm trying to keep her in bed,' he said, 'but I feel like King Canute trying to stop the tide.'

Liz grinned. 'I brought these for her.' She showed him the fruit. 'And this for you.' A bottle of gin. 'A little bird told me it was your favourite, and I thought you might need it.'

'Thank God.' Irwin took the bottle gratefully. 'I'm all out. Come in, come in and take your coat off.'

She looked around the kitchen. It could have fallen straight from the pages of a Dickens novel, with a huge black range and open shelving lined with jars of preserves. The gas stove was more modern but still decades old, almost as ancient as the ones she'd taken out of her own cottages. She saw pastry rolled out on the table.

'What are you baking?'

'Apple pie. I had a glut of apples in my garden this year and thought I'd keep myself busy. Not that I should have worried about that.'

'IS THAT LIZ I CAN HEAR?'

Irwin pulled a face. 'You'd better go up and see her, or she'll come down.'

Liz shrugged off her coat and took the fruit basket upstairs. She found Iris on the second floor, tucked into an iron bed topped with a threadbare patchwork quilt. Iris's eyes widened when she saw the basket in her hands.

'OH, IS THAT FRUIT? LOVELY! I LIKE TO KEEP MYSELF REGULAR.'

'How're you feeling?' asked Liz.

The old lady sniffed. 'I TOLD YOU IN THE HOSPITAL. THERE'S NOTHING WRONG WITH ME.'

'It can't hurt you to stay in bed for a few days, though, can it?'

'HE'S KEEPING ME A PRISONER UP HERE.'

'He's just trying to do what's best.'

'BEST FOR HIM, NOT BEST FOR ME.'

Liz thought a change of subject was in order. 'Have you seen the article in the *Bugle*?'

'I HAVE. THEY GOT IT WRONG. GORDON DOESN'T LIVE IN STARFISH COTTAGE, HE LIVES IN STAR*BOARD* COTTAGE. YOU'D THINK DONNIE SATTERTHWAITE WOULD HAVE GOT THAT RIGHT, AT LEAST, LIVING RIGHT NEXT TO HIM.'

'It said in the article that Donnie heard the howling too.'

'IT DID, AND THEN LOOK WHAT HAPPENED. I TOLD YOU, DIDN'T I? I TOLD YOU SOMEONE WAS GOING TO DIE.' Iris sniffed. 'I NEVER LIKED THE MAN. HE NEVER PUT HIS RUBBISH OUT ON BIN NIGHT. IT MADE THE YARD SMELL SOMETHING TERRIBLE.'

'He didn't deserve to die, though, did he?' said Liz, slightly appalled.

'SUPPOSE NOT.' Iris lowered the volume a little. 'NO ONE DESERVES TO GO LIKE THAT. MY BLOOD RUNS COLD JUST THINKING ABOUT IT.'

Liz spent another forty minutes with Iris, mostly speculating about Donnie Satterthwaite's death and who might have killed him. Afterwards she went downstairs, and Irwin showed her to the door.

'Are you sure you can't stay longer?' he pleaded. 'The pie's almost ready.'

The aroma coming from the stove was delicious, but Liz shook her head.

'I don't like leaving Nelson on his own for too long.' In fact, Nelson was very happy with his own company for two or three hours, as long as he'd been outside first, but he was useful as an excuse. Liz's eardrums had taken as much as they could bear.

Irwin nodded. 'Thanks for coming to see her. And for the gin. Much appreciated.'

Liz stepped out into the yard. After Irwin shut the door, it took a few moments for her eyes to adjust to the gloom. She was just about to head across to the gate when a darker shape detached itself from the doorway of Satterthwaite's cottage. She jumped, but recovered when she saw who it was.

'Constable Williams! You almost gave me a heart attack.'

'Sorry, Mrs Mac.' Bill Williams, known to some of his fellow officers as Double Bill, didn't smile. Liz looked more closely at him. His long face was agitated.

'Is there something the matter?'

He shifted from foot to foot, clearly debating whether to tell her. In the end he seemed to come to a decision.

'Are you any good with birds?'

'What?'

'With birds. I think it's a blackbird, although it's hard to tell with all the soot and all.'

Liz stared at him.

His shoulders sagged. 'The inspector told me to come down here and make sure the scene was secure. But there's a bird in there. It must have fallen down the chimney. It's flapping around, making a terrible mess. I don't know what to do.'

'Why not call the inspector and tell her?'

'I can't do that!'

'It's hardly your fault, is it?' said Liz.

'No... but you know what she's like. I'd sooner try to sort it out myself... only...'

'Only?'

'I *really* hate birds.' He shuddered. 'Nasty, bony, flappy things.'

Liz looked at him. The best course of action really was for him to call for help, but if he wasn't willing to do that, the situation did have advantages. She might get the chance to look into Satterthwaite's cottage after all.

'Okay,' she said. 'I'll give you a hand. It'll be easier with two of us.'

He looked simultaneously relieved and appalled. 'I'm not going in there again,' he said. 'I can't.'

Liz frowned. Was he really going to let her go into a crime scene on her own? Apparently, he was.

Birds did occasionally fall down the chimney in her cottages – a natural hazard with big eighteenth-century flues. Liz's usual course of action was to close the curtains at every window except one and then open that window. The bird tended to head for the light and freedom. But, of course, that only worked in the daytime. She would have to use plan B.

'I need a net,' she said. 'Or something to throw over it.'

They hunted around the yard, using the constable's flashlight. Eventually they found a piece of sacking that had been used to cover an old barrel.

'That'll do.' She took her coat off, as she didn't want to get it dirty. 'Is the electricity on?'

Williams looked at her blankly.

'The electricity in the cottage? I can't catch the bird in the dark.'

'Oh, yes. Yes, it is. The light switch is on the left.'

Unusually for a Whitby cottage, the front door of Satterthwaite's cottage didn't open directly into the kitchen, but into a narrow hall that led to a staircase at the far end. Liz switched on the light. There was nothing in the hall except for a hanging rail of coats. Liz went to the only door that she guessed was the kitchen. She pushed it open and switched on the light.

The kitchen was surprisingly modern, with sleek, black units and a granite work counter. There were no soft touches, no curtains at the window, no cushions on the sofa or ornaments. Definitely the home of a bachelor. It was tidy, with only a few things out of place – the door to the wood-burning stove was slightly ajar, and there was an opened packet of digestive biscuits on the counter. Liz was surprised at that. She thought the police would have taken the biscuits as evidence, seeing as Satterthwaite had been poisoned.

She could hear fluttering, but couldn't see the bird. There was evidence of it, though – little splatters of bird poo here and there on the wooden floor and on the counters. It had been in the cottage a while.

The fluttering came again, and she realised it was coming from the corner of the room, behind the sofa.

She crept towards it, sacking at the ready. And stopped. On the wall under the windowsill was a paw print, just as Kevin had described. It was dark brown, like dried blood, but his description hadn't prepared her for just how huge it was. The main part, the pad of the foot, must have been six or seven inches across. There was no way a dog could have made it. No ordinary dog, anyway. Liz shivered.

She peered over the back of the sofa and spotted the bird, a huddle of feathers tucked right into the corner. It *was* a blackbird – its yellow beak gave it away. Trying not to scare it, she pulled the sofa away from the wall, then knelt down and gently covered it with the sacking. Easy. When she picked it up, she could feel it trembling through the coarse material. She couldn't imagine why Williams had made a fuss over such a harmless little thing! But phobias weren't rational. She herself had a blind, unreasoning fear of clowns – coulrophobia – and you couldn't get anything more innocuous than clowns, could you? The very first nightmare she could remember had been of a clown, with spinning crosses for eyes. Later in life, she realised it had probably been prompted by the clown on the BBC test card, but that hadn't made it any less scary. It had stayed with her all her life.

She was carrying the bird carefully to the door when something caught her eye. There was something white poking out at floor level that had fallen down the gap between the kitchen cabinet and the fridge. It had obviously come off the wall – she could see a nail hole there. She carefully transferred the bird into one hand so she had her other hand free to pull the object out. It was a calendar. The month of October was filled with football fixtures, a dentist appointment, and a reminder to put the recycling out. Satterthwaite had been killed on the twenty-first of October. There *was* something marked that day – *MD coming tea 6pm*. She wasn't sure of the exact timings, but the fact that he'd invited someone for tea on the evening he'd been poisoned surely had to be significant? The bird stirred, reminding her of the task in hand. She put the calendar on the kitchen counter and took the bird outside.

Constable Williams stood well back as she released the blackbird. It fluttered along the cobbles for a yard or two, making Williams squeak, before finding its bearings and flying up into the night sky. Liz watched it go with a feeling of satisfaction.

'I can't thank you enough, Mrs Mac,' said Williams. 'I don't know what I'd have done if I hadn't bumped into you.'

'No problem.' She put her coat on again. 'Are you going to tell the inspector?'

'I won't mention you, but I suppose I'll have to tell her about the bird. It's made quite a mess.' Williams looked glum. 'She'll probably blame me for it.'

Liz felt sorry for him. 'If you want to get back into her good books, I have a suggestion.'

'Oh?' Williams perked up.

'Tell her to look at Satterthwaite's calendar.'

'His calendar?'

'On the counter beside the fridge. Have a look at it yourself before you lock up.' She started towards the gate, then turned back. 'Oh, and I'd close the wood burner door too, unless you want another bird getting in.'

5

'I'm Neville, and this is my wife, Jackie. Pleased to meet you, Mrs McLuckie.'

Liz shook the hand of the man standing on her doorstep. With his ruddy cheeks, stocky build and thinning sandy hair, Neville Robertson looked more like a country farmer than a Goth. Actually, he was neither – he was an IT manager from Manchester. His wife, Jackie, beamed at her and shook her hand vigorously. She was a tiny woman with dark eyes, no more than five feet tall, and swamped by the oversized, white puffer jacket she was wearing. She looked a bit like a mouse that had fallen into a meringue. Liz pushed the unkind thought away.

'How was your trip?' she asked.

'There was a bit of a delay with the train at York, but it wasn't too bad,' said Neville. 'I can't tell you how much we've been looking forward to this. It's our first time, you know.'

Liz guessed he meant they were Goth Week virgins. She smiled. 'Mine too. Come on, I'll show you round.'

She led them next door and showed them around Kipper Cottage.

'Very nice!' said Neville. Liz had to admit that the kitchen, with its big inglenook fireplace, original stone floor and new curtains, did look lovely. She'd also put a jar of pansies on the table, as a welcoming touch.

'We'll be very comfortable here, won't we, Jackie?'

'We will. Can we light a fire if we want?'

'Of course. There's firelighters, matches and kindling in the basket, and more logs under the stairs. The hot water's from a combi boiler, so it'll be there whenever you need it. If there's anything else you need, don't be shy to ask. As you know, I'm only next door.'

'Thank you.' Neville hesitated. 'Is Neptune Yard far from here?'

Liz looked at him.

'We read about the dog,' he explained. 'The demon dog?'

In the six days since Iris's sighting, the national newspapers had picked up the story. Satterthwaite's death had been the icing on the cake – the media seemed to be much less bothered by the fact he'd been murdered, more interested that his death had fulfilled the Barghest prophecy.

'It's just at the end of the street. By the bottom of the abbey steps,' said Liz. 'You passed it on your way here.'

She wasn't sure she should have told them. Iris wouldn't get much rest if she had dozens of demon hunters traipsing in and out of her yard.

Jackie gave Neville an excited look. 'I can't believe it, Nev! The Barghest appearing just in time for our visit!' She turned to Liz. 'Look what I've bought.' She took off her meringue jacket and showed Liz what she was wearing underneath – a grey T-shirt with an illustration of a howling dog. Underneath, it said *The Barghest, Whitby* in a spooky font. Liz was impressed. Some local entrepreneur had really pulled out the stops to get it made in time.

'I bought it at a café on the way here,' said Jackie, 'and changed into it in their toilet.'

'A café?' echoed Liz.

Jackie nodded. 'The Full Moon, I think it was called.'

LIZ HAD NEVER SEEN the café so busy. Peering through one of the windows, she could see it was heaving with a flock of black-clad customers. Every table was taken, and there was also a queue of people at the counter. She blinked. Was she imagining things, or was that Iris's favourite green hat she could see in the middle of the melee?

It was.

Liz fought her way in and saw Iris sitting at her usual table, surrounded by a group of admirers. Some were dressed in Victorian-style costume, others simply dressed in black, but they were all hanging on the old lady's words as if she were the Dalai Lama.

Iris was clearly in her element.

'IT WAS JUST STANDING THERE,' she shouted. 'STARING AT ME WITH ITS BIG YELLOW EYES.'

Yellow eyes? That detail was new.

Someone spotted Liz over the top of the crowd and waved.

'Want a Barghest T-shirt, Mrs Mac?' shouted Niall. 'Only twenty-five quid! Fifteen, to you!' He was serving the queue of customers that stretched out the door. Before she could answer, she felt someone grab her elbow and steer her through the beaded curtain into the passage beyond, which was piled with boxes and bags of vegetables.

'It's brilliant, isn't it?' gasped Tilly. Her face was pink and sweating, but her grin was huge. She was wearing the crimson cape Liz had made for her.

'It is,' agreed Liz. 'I've never seen it so busy in here. But... shouldn't Iris be resting?'

'I tried to tell her... but you know Iris.'

Liz pulled a face. She did. Wild horses wouldn't have kept her away from an audience.

'We've agreed I'll give her a percentage of the T-shirt takings. Niall's on commission too.'

'How did you make them up so fast?'

'Louie at the print shop... you know Louie? Big guy, dreadlocks. He pulled an all-nighter.'

'Excuse me.' Grazyna squeezed past them, carrying a tray of bottled lagers.

'Did the council change their minds about the licence too?' asked Liz. 'That's great!'

'It is, isn't it?' But Tilly didn't meet her eye. *Odd.*

'Table eight, ready!' shouted Mags, invisibly, from the kitchen.

'If you want a cuppa, you can come in and help yourself,' said Tilly. 'No charge.'

'That's okay,' said Liz. 'I'll get out of your way. Catch you later.'

As Tilly headed into the kitchen, Liz made her way back out through the curtain into the café.

'IT STARED AT ME WITH ITS BIG, YELLOW, GLOWING EYES, AND EVERYTHING WENT COLD!' Iris was onto a fresh set of listeners, with new embellishments. 'LIKE THE DEVIL HIMSELF HAD BREATHED ON ME!' She waved her bottle of lager for emphasis. 'THE DEVIL HIMSELF!'

Liz winced. She hoped the old lady wasn't heading for another angina attack. Did Irwin know where she was? And another thing bothered her – why had Tilly looked so sheepish when she'd mentioned the drinks licence? She should be really happy about it.

Just as she was squeezing out the door, Liz spotted Dora Spackle sitting at one of the corner tables. That surprised her. Dora rarely came into the café, and Liz didn't think ghost stories would be her thing. From the sour look on her face, she clearly wasn't enjoying Iris's performance.

Back out on the street, Liz took a deep lungful of air. A passing gentleman in a top hat and tails gave her a nod of greeting. He was accompanied by two ladies in pink-striped gowns with black-feathered hats, carrying hatboxes. One of the hatboxes had a severed head in it.

Whitby Goth Festival had definitely arrived.

THE BELLS in St Mary's Church on the clifftop above Gull Cottage chimed seven am, rousing Liz from a deep slumber. She lay in bed for a while, dipping in and out of sleep and thinking about Mark. The mornings were always the worst. During the day, when she was busy with other things, she could almost forget he was gone. But the moment she opened her eyes, grief ambushed her. She didn't think that would ever change.

Scratch, scratch, scratch.

Her alarm clock – otherwise known as Nelson – went off downstairs in the kitchen, reminding her it was time to get up.

It was still quite dark when she took Nelson for his morning walk along the clifftop. The air was still, heavy with overripe vegetation and woodsmoke –the scents of autumn. Unsurprisingly, they had the abbey steps and graveyard to themselves.

Liz wandered down the path that skirted St Mary's Church, while Nelson hunted for rabbits in the long grass. She could just make out the ruins of the abbey in the pearling light. Only the eastern wall was still standing, gaunt and massive, punctuated by narrow windows. It was visible from miles away, silhouetted on the clifftop, and had become the iconic image of the town, used on every poster and tourist leaflet. Liz wondered what Saint Hilda, its most famous medieval abbess, would say about the hordes of Goths invading the town today. No doubt she'd have taken it in her stride. Hilda had been a very practical woman and would certainly have recognised an opportunity for trade when she saw one. Much like Tilly Fairweather with her Barghest T-shirts. Liz grinned at her mental coupling of the reformed burglar and the Christian saint. They had more in common than people might imagine.

The path wound between gravestones that leaned drunkenly into each other. Liz shivered, thinking of Donnie Satterthwaite. From Kevin's silence on the subject, she guessed the police had drawn a blank in the investigation so far. It really was astonishing that someone could murder in cold blood, in such a dramatic way, right in the centre of the town, with no one hearing or seeing a thing. Had Donnie known his killer? Was it the mysterious 'MD' marked on his calendar? She wondered if Constable Williams had pointed it out to DI Flint yet. She imagined he had. If Liz had been the one who'd told her, Flint wouldn't have taken the clue seriously. Flint didn't like her very much, one of those 'loathing at first sight' things, not helped by the fact they'd trodden on each other's toes in the murder investigation during the summer.

St Mary's Church struck eight thirty am. A hollow, mournful sound.

Liz whistled for Nelson. 'Come on, we have work to do.'

IT WASN'T usual for breakfast to be included in short-term holiday lets, but Neville had asked if Liz could provide a continental breakfast during their stay, and she had agreed. It was easy enough to do.

She gave Nelson his breakfast, then went to the table where she had everything ready: croissants, fruit jam, marmalade and honey, cereal, muesli, bread for toasting, fresh fruit and a carton of milk. She put everything into a basket, tucked a tea towel over it, and took it next door.

She knocked quietly. No answer. They must still be asleep. She carefully opened the door with her key and slipped the basket inside.

When she let herself back into Gull Cottage, Niall was up and about, banging around in the kitchen.

'Have we no bread?' he complained.

'I've just taken the last of it next door. I think there's a loaf in the icebox. You'll have to toast it from frozen.'

Niall opened the fridge and prised the door of the icebox open. He had to wrestle to free the loaf from the appliance's icy grip.

'This fridge is knackered,' he said.

'The whole kitchen's knackered,' agreed Liz cheerfully. 'But Kipper was the priority. What are your plans for today?'

Niall hacked at the frozen loaf with a bread knife. 'I dunno. I thought I might take some of Tilly's T-shirts over to the pier and see if I can sell them there.'

'Don't let the police catch you.'

He looked at her blankly.

'You don't have a licence?'

'Ah, don't worry, I'll keep moving.' He jammed a couple of slices into the toaster.

'Talking of licences,' said Liz, 'has Tilly mentioned anything to you about her drinks licence?'

'Only that the council had changed its mind. Why?'

'No reason.'

'What about you?' he asked. 'What are you doing today?'

'I might go to the book signing at Poole's.'

'Yeah?'

'Emma Summers.'

Niall was impressed. 'My ma fecking *loves* Emma Summers.'

'Did you know she lives in Whitby?'

'No way!'

Emma Summers was an actress who'd had middling success in TV, but then, in her forties, had found unexpected fame in a series of low-budget British horror films that had become cult classics. She was always a favourite with festival-goers, and this year she was likely to be more popular than ever.

'She's launching her new autobiography today,' said Liz. '*Blood Sister*, I think it's called.' It was a reference to Summers' famous vampire character.

'My ma would love that for Christmas.' Niall gave her his most beguiling smile. 'If you're going, can you get me a copy? I'll pay you for it.'

6

'Who would you like me to dedicate it to?' Like most actresses, Emma Summers was very different in the flesh to how she looked on the screen. Her most famous role – Alyssa the Vampyre – was powerful and charismatic. In reality, Emma was much less imposing. She was delicately built and dark featured, with a fine network of lines on her face, artfully covered with make-up. Liz reckoned she was in her late sixties and still beautiful.

'Kathleen.'

Emma bent her glossy head to her task. There was a long queue in the bookshop behind Liz, and there had been a lot of people in front of her. Many of them were Goths, but there were quite a few locals too. Grazyna was one of them, waiting her turn farther back in the queue with a copy of *Blood Sisters* in her hand. Eryk and Lukasz were sitting on the floor by one of the bookcases, looking bored. Liz wondered why they weren't at school, then realised it was probably half-term.

Emma handed her back the signed book, and Liz gave her another.

'Just a signature on this one, please.'

Emma nodded and added her flourish to the flysheet.

'Thank you.' Liz took her book and made way for the next fan in the queue.

The door opened. Constable Williams stepped in.

No one in the bookshop took any notice... except Eryk and Lukasz, whose sudden movement caught Liz's attention. They jumped up, panic-stricken, looking for an exit. The only way out was past Williams. They spotted the spiral staircase up to the mezzanine level and made a dash for it. In the blink of an eye they had vanished. Liz stepped back and peered up at the mezzanine. No sign of the boys. Were they lying on the floor? Liz looked at Grazyna, but she was deep in conversation with the woman next to her in the queue and hadn't noticed the peculiar behaviour of her sons. Neither had Constable Williams, who'd taken a copy of *Blood Sister* to the till.

Liz put her own books in her bag and headed for the staircase. When she got to the top, there was still no sign of the boys. She spotted a freestanding bookshelf on wheels. The only hiding place. As she suspected, the twins were huddled behind it.

'Okay, you two. What's going on?'

They looked up at her, dark eyes wide. Lukasz was the first to recover.

'Nothing, Mrs McLuckie.' He stood up.

'So why are you hiding?'

'We're not hiding. We're just having a rest, aren't we, Eryk?' Lukasz looked at his brother for confirmation. Eryk nodded vigorously.

'Sorry,' said Liz, 'but I don't believe you.'

The boys said nothing.

'If you won't tell me, perhaps you'd like to tell Constable Williams?' Looking over the mezzanine railing, Liz could see that Williams had taken his book and joined the back of the signing queue. Bless him. Most of his fellow officers would have taken it straight to the front. 'Shall I call him up?'

'No! Don't do that!' Both boys panicked.

Liz looked at them seriously. 'You can't tell me it's nothing. I saw how you were with Detective Ossett in the café yesterday, and now with Constable Williams. There's something going on, and I don't want your poor mother to have to deal with it.'

The boys stared at her, dismayed.

'Why don't we sit down, and you can tell me all about it?' She took a seat on the small chesterfield sofa provided for book browsers, and waited. Her chill attitude told the boys she had all day if necessary.

Eryk and Lukasz eyed each other. Eryk nodded to his brother, whose shoulders slumped.

'Do you promise not to tell?' asked Eryk.

'I'm not promising anything. Tell me what's going on, and we'll see.'

They came to sit on the floor in front of her, then looked at each other in silent communication. Where to start?

'You know the dog?' said Lukasz. 'The Barghest?'

Liz nodded.

He took a deep breath. 'It's us.'

She stared at him. *What?*

'We gave Mrs Gladwell a heart attack. But we didn't mean to.'

'And...' began Eryk. Lukasz cut him off with a glare.

'And?' prompted Liz.

Lukasz sighed. 'And we made the paw print in Mr Satterthwaite's cottage.'

'He was a horrible man,' added Eryk, 'but we didn't want him to die.'

Liz looked at each of the boys in turn, her mind whirling.

'I think you should start at the beginning.'

They settled themselves more comfortably on the floor. Lukas took a deep breath.

'A couple of weeks ago, on a Thursday...'

'It was Friday,' Eryk interrupted.

'No, it wasn't.'

'It was, because we had fish and chips, remember?'

Liz controlled her impatience. 'Don't worry about what day it was,' she said. 'Just tell me what happened.'

Lukasz began. 'We saw Mr Satterthwaite put a letter in our post box.'

'Mum had asked us to get the post because she was at work.'

'She gives us the key.'

'We saw him put the letter in the box.'

'He was acting really weird and ran away when he saw us.'

Eryk corrected. 'He didn't run. He just walked fast.'

Liz cut in again. 'One at a time!' She was getting dizzy.

'Let me tell her,' said Lukasz. 'I'm the oldest.'

'By about three seconds.'

'But still the oldest.'

Eryk folded his arms and pulled a face, but let his brother continue.

'We took the post upstairs. It was mostly bills...'

'Brown envelopes,' explained Eryk.

Lukasz glared at him. 'Bills, like I said. Except for one. It had mum's name on it, but no stamp. We guessed it was the one Mr Satterthwaite had put in the box.' The boys exchanged a guilty look.

'You opened it?' said Liz.

'We thought he might be crushing on Mum,' said Lukasz sheepishly. 'We wanted to know.'

'For a laugh,' said Eryk.

'You're not supposed to open other people's post,' said Liz.
'But... okay. What was in it?'

Lukasz looked at Eryk. An unspoken question. Eryk nodded.
Lukasz reached into his jacket pocket and pulled out a piece of
paper, which he gave to Liz. It had a few lines of writing on it.

*I want another £500. Pay it in the usual way, or I will
reveal your secret. You have until October 31st.*

Short, but not so sweet.

'We have no idea what Mum's secret is,' said Lukasz, 'but
we didn't want her to get into trouble.'

'She's our mum,' added Eryk. 'She can be a bit grumpy,
but we love her.'

'Of course you do.' Liz met their concerned eyes, and her
heart went out to them both. As far as she knew, their father
was long gone, but she had no idea if he'd died, or he and
Grazyna had just parted ways. 'So what did you do?'

'We sneaked into Satterthwaite's cottage,' said Lukasz,
'while he was asleep.'

'It was easy. His door wasn't locked.'

Liz nodded. That wasn't unusual in the town. It was old
fashioned and more than a bit naive, but comforting in a way.

Lukasz continued, 'We looked around for anything he
might have about Mum. About her secret... evidence... you
know.'

Liz nodded. She wasn't above a bit of snooping for
evidence herself when necessary.

'But we couldn't find anything. Except this.' Eryk reached
into his pocket and took out another sheet of paper. This one
was smaller than the blackmail note and green. It looked as if
it had been torn from a memo pad of some kind. On it was a
list of names. *Grazyna Polonsky* was right at the top.

'What did you do then?' asked Liz.

'We wanted to scare him,' said Lukasz. 'So we painted a paw print on the wall.'

'In brown poster paint, to look like mud.'

Liz almost smiled. The police thought it was dried blood.

'And then we went into the yard and howled.' Eryk lifted his chin and took a deep breath, about to demonstrate, when his brother dug him in the ribs.

'Not here, idiot!'

Eryk looked embarrassed. He'd forgotten where he was.

'We are pretty good at howling,' said Lukasz. 'We never thought that Mrs Gladwell might hear us and be scared. We never meant for her to have a heart attack. Just that horrible man.'

Eryk cut in. 'But we didn't kill him.'

'If the police find out we were in his cottage, they might think we did,' said Lukasz.

'You won't tell anyone, will you?' implored Eryk.

Liz hesitated.

'Please, Mrs Mac,' said Lukasz. 'We'll get into so much trouble.'

'Please!'

Liz capitulated. 'Okay.'

'Do you promise?' said Lukasz.

'Cross your heart and hope to die?'

She looked at the two anxious faces and gave in.

'Okay.'

7

On her way back to Gull Cottage, Liz bumped into Neville and Jackie. She didn't recognise them at first, until Neville called out to her.

'Mrs McLuckie!' He was wearing a nineteenth-century waistcoat, trews and cravat. His hair had changed from sandy to black, with a silver streak at the front, and his shirtsleeves were bloody to the elbows. Jackie cut a neat figure in a low-cut, black Victorian dress, complete with pillbox hat and a veil.

'Sweeny Todd and Mrs Lovett,' she guessed.

'Exactly!' beamed Neville.

'You look magnificent.'

'Thank you!'

'We're just on our way to the book signing,' said Jackie. 'Would you like us to get you a copy?'

'I've just got one, thanks.'

'Are we too late?' asked Jackie anxiously.

'I shouldn't think so. There was still quite a queue when I left.'

'Excellent!' beamed Neville. 'See you later!'

Nobody looked at them twice as they hurried off down the street. They blended perfectly into the extraordinary crowd. As Liz watched them go, her stomach lurched. A clown had emerged from one of the shops nearby. She averted her eyes quickly.

She supposed she shouldn't really be shocked to see one at the festival – she wasn't the only person who thought they were the stuff of nightmares. Liz held her breath until the grinning, white-faced horror had gone into another shop, then continued on her way.

When she got in, she gave Nelson a chewy treat and put the kettle on. She needed to think.

The boys' confession had put her in a dilemma. She shouldn't withhold information from the police – Satterthwaite was a blackmailer, and that very probably had something to do with his murder. On the other hand, she didn't want to get the boys or Grazyna into trouble. She took Satterthwaite's blackmail letter and the list of names from her pocket and sat down to study them.

The letter said 'another £500'. Grazyna had already paid Satterthwaite at least once. She didn't earn a fortune at the café, and £500 was a lot of money. Whatever he'd found out about her, it had to be something serious.

Grazyna was at the top of the list, followed by several other names: CHARLIE JOHNSON, PHILIP NETHERGATE, MARTY DAVIDSON, EMMA SUMMERS and GILLIAN GARRAWAY.

Liz gasped at the two names she knew – Emma Summers and Gillian Garraway. What had they done to get their names put on a blackmail list?

Liz corrected herself. She was making an assumption. It might not be a blackmail list at all, but something perfectly harmless. If so, the names had to have something in common. But what? She read through them again and realised she knew them all – not personally, but by reputation. Charlie Johnson was a local councillor, Nethergate a businessman who owned most of the amusement arcades on the harbour, and Marty Davidson owned the Crab and Cockle restaurant on the market square. And, of course, there was Emma Summers. She couldn't think of a single thing that might connect all six. She looked again at the names. Marty Davidson. Could he be the mysterious 'MD' Satterthwaite had invited to tea?

The kettle whistled on the stove. Liz put the papers carefully back in her pocket. She wouldn't tell Kevin about them just yet. She wanted to think of a way to protect Grazyna and Gillian from any potential repercussions that might occur when she did.

THURSDAY NIGHT WAS MAH-JONG NIGHT. Usually. That week, however, they'd moved it to Monday because of their various commitments during the festival.

'I wasn't sure you'd make it,' said Liz to Kevin as they set the table for supper in Benedict's conservatory. Benedict had made a lamb tagine that was filling his big house with the tantalising scent of spices and apricots. 'I thought you'd be too busy, what with the murder and everything.'

'Mmm,' said Kevin noncommittally.

'Aren't you making progress?'

'Not really. No one really liked Satterthwaite. The whole town could have done it. Flint is tearing her hair out.'

'Had anyone searched his cottage?'

Kevin looked affronted. 'Of course.'

'I don't mean you lot. I mean whoever killed him.'

'What would they be looking for?'

'I don't know.' Liz shrugged. 'But someone killed him for a reason, didn't they?'

'There was no sign of a search. It was very tidy.'

That was true. Liz remembered from her own visit. 'And nothing stolen?'

'Not as far as we can tell. Even his laptop was untouched.' He gave her a hard look. 'I hope you're not thinking of getting involved?'

'I'm only trying to help. Perhaps he invited someone that evening? Did he have a diary of some kind?' She was fishing to see if Constable Williams had mentioned the calendar.

Kevin narrowed his eyes at her.

'Hello, my darlings!' Tilly bounced into the conservatory in a cloud of patchouli oil. She was wearing a long tweed skirt and purple mohair jumper. Anyone else would have looked like an eccentric bag lady, but somehow Tilly just looked cool. She dipped a finger into the bowl of yoghurt dressing to taste it.

'Tills!' snapped Kevin. 'Everyone else has to eat that, you know.'

Tilly just grinned. She and Kevin had an easy-going, banterous relationship, very like brother and sister. Liz supposed it was because they'd been at school together.

'Here we go.' Benedict carried a tureen out of the kitchen and put it carefully on the table. 'Sit down. Dig in. There are some naans under the foil.'

He always cooked supper for the four of them before their first game, and Liz often helped him with the kitchen prep. It was the only time she ever had him to herself, and she savoured it. Gillian was never there because she didn't play mah-jong. Liz felt only slightly guilty for being glad about that.

Everyone helped themselves to tagine.

'This looks awesome,' said Tilly.

'I was wondering,' began Liz, 'have any of you ever eaten at the Crab and Cockle?'

Benedict nodded. 'The food's very good.'

'What's the chef's name?' asked Liz disingenuously.

'Marty Davidson,' said Benedict. 'I think he owns the restaurant too. They got a Michelin star last year.'

'Marty Davidson.' Liz put only the slightest emphasis on the *M* and the *D*. Kevin's eyes flashed to her. Liz turned her attention to her food, satisfied that Constable Williams had done his work.

'How are the sales of your T-shirts going?' Benedict asked Tilly. 'I saw Niall on the harbour with them this afternoon.'

'Really good, thanks. We've sold dozens and dozens. It cost a fair bit to get them made, but I think we'll make some money.'

'And you got your drinks licence too,' said Liz. 'That's great.'

'Mmm.' Tilly took a naan bread and bit into it. Liz looked at her. There was *definitely* something off there.

'It's really lucky,' said Benedict, 'that the Barghest made an appearance in time for the festival.'

Everyone nodded. Liz chewed her mouthful of tagine thoughtfully. His words had made her realise something – the Barghest *had* made an appearance, hadn't it? Iris hadn't just *heard* the twins' howling, she'd *seen* the dog too. Or so she'd thought. What was that about?

'The paw print in Satterthwaite's cottage is really spooky.' Tilly shivered. In spite of Flint's best efforts to keep it secret, the *Bugle* had found out about the paw print, and their excited report on it had fanned the flames of Barghest fever even further. 'I wonder whose blood it was.'

'It wasn't blood,' said Liz, without thinking. She looked up and saw Kevin's gaze had locked onto her.

'Oh?' he challenged her, his tone deceptively casual.

She shrugged. 'I don't know for sure. I'm just speculating.'

Kevin turned his attention back to his supper. But Liz knew the damage was done.

After supper they cleared away the dishes and then played three games of mah-jong. They took a break and then played another two. Liz played particularly badly, waiting for Kevin's axe to fall. Before she knew it, it was time to go home. She was starting to think she might have gotten away with her slip, when Kevin made his move.

'I'll run you two home if you like?' he said.

'No, it's...' began Liz.

'That's great!' cut in Tilly. 'Thanks, Kev.'

Liz knew she'd been outmanoeuvred.

Kevin dropped Tilly in Church Street, then drove on to Henrietta Street in silence. Liz practically leapt out of the car before it had stopped.

'Thanks!'

'Not so fast!' He spoke through the car window. 'We need to talk. I'll be in shortly.'

By the time he'd found somewhere to park the car, Liz had put the gas fire on to warm the cottage up, and made them both a mug of cocoa. She sat him down and explained about her adventure in Neptune Yard with the blackbird.

'So let me get this straight,' he said. 'You told Williams about the calendar?'

Liz looked at him across the table. 'I'm sure one of you would've spotted it eventually.'

'Well, thank you for that vote of confidence,' said Kevin sourly. He sipped his cocoa. 'I can't believe he let you into Satterthwaite's cottage.'

'He *really* doesn't like birds. You won't tell Flint, will you? I don't want him to get into trouble.'

Kevin sighed. 'I suppose not... You think Marty Davidson might be the MD on the calendar?'

'I've no idea.'

'So why did you mention him? You were very particular. Marty Davidson.' He emphasised the *M* and the *D*.

'That was a bit heavy-handed, wasn't it?'

'Just a bit... So?'

She couldn't tell him Marty Davidson's name was on the list. 'Because he's the only MD in town I can think of. There are bound to be lots of others, though.'

Kevin looked unconvinced. 'How do you know the paw print isn't blood?'

Liz bit her lip. That wasn't so easy to explain.

He pressed on. 'The results only came back from the lab this morning.'

Liz knew she had to give him something, but didn't want to tell him Satterthwaite was blackmailing Grazyna and Gillian. Not yet at least. She had no choice but to grass on the boys.

'Lukasz and Eryk painted it. With poster paint.'

Whatever Kevin had been expecting, that wasn't it. 'What?'

'They thought Satterthwaite fancied Grazyna and decided to play a trick on him.' Not too far from the truth. 'So they crept into his house and made the paw print.'

'They broke in?'

'The door wasn't locked. Apparently.'

'What about the howling?'

'Also them.'

'So the dog had nothing to do with Satterthwaite's death?'

'You didn't really think it did, did you?'

Kevin blushed. Liz grinned at him. For people who prided themselves on their no-nonsense approach to life, Yorkshire men could be very superstitious.

He changed the subject. 'I can't keep that to myself. I have to tell Flint.'

'Really? It was just a prank.'

'A prank that's muddying the waters of a murder investigation.'

He had a point. She didn't like the idea of DI Flint repri-
manding the boys, but it was better than her grilling Gillian
and Grazyna about why they were being blackmailed. Liz
knew she would have to tell Kevin about the blackmail
sooner rather than later, but she didn't want to drop her
friends in it just yet. The question was, would the boys tell
Flint about it?

She heard a key in the door. Niall clattered in, wearing his
Bride of Frankenstein costume, wide-eyed and dishevelled
with excitement.

'You'll never guess what's happened!' he gasped.

They stared at him. They had no idea.

'The Barghest is back!'

8

The next day all of Whitby was agog with the news: the Barghest had been heard again, this time by dozens of people in the Duke of York. Excited customers had flung open the windows when they'd heard the eerie howling, but the darkness had made it impossible to pinpoint exactly where the howls were coming from. They'd only lasted thirty seconds or so.

Neville and Jackie pounced on Liz when she delivered their breakfast.

'Is it true?' asked Neville. 'Is the Barghest back?'

'That's what I heard.' She didn't want to burst their bubble by telling them the ghostly dog wasn't real. She was surprised Lukasz and Eryk had reprised their role, however. It was going to get them into even more trouble with Detective Inspector Flint.

'Is someone else going to die, do you think?' asked Jackie.

'Let's hope not.' Liz decided to change the subject. 'I couldn't get any marmalade this morning. I hope raspberry jam is okay?'

'I don't suppose you heard it, did you?' asked Neville.

'No, sorry.' She decided not to tell them that Niall had. After he and the pub customers had heard the howls, they had searched the two 'ghauts', the alleyways that flanked the pub and led down to the shore, but found nothing. It sounded like the twins had had a close call.

'We might go down to the Duke of York later to take a look for ourselves,' said Neville. 'We've already been to Neptune Yard, but saw nothing.'

'The Duke does a very nice pub lunch,' said Liz. 'I can recommend it.'

'That's what we'll do, then, eh, Jackie? Kill two birds with one stone.'

Jackie agreed enthusiastically. 'This is even better than we expected! A real live haunting!'

'Do demons haunt?' mused Neville. 'Or is that only ghosts?'

Liz had no idea. She left the excited pair to their breakfast and returned next door.

Niall was still in bed. He wasn't usually a late sleeper, but the drama had obviously worn him out. Liz tried not to make too much noise as she washed up her own breakfast things and the mugs from the night before. She regretted having to tell Kevin about the twins and the paw print, but she'd really had no choice. She hoped the boys wouldn't mention blackmail to Flint.

After she'd made herself a cup of tea, she sat at the table and looked around the kitchen of Gull Cottage. It was in quite a state compared to Kipper. The walls were covered in cheap wooden panelling, and there was a horrible, swirly-patterned orange carpet, circa 1970. If she was lucky, there would be an inglenook fireplace hidden behind the panelling, like there had been in Kipper Cottage. When the festival was over, she intended to take a crowbar to it to investigate.

Ideally, she'd like to have Gull Cottage ready for guests by the spring. She wasn't sure what she would do then. She might just rent out one of the cottages and continue to live in the other, or she might rent out both and find herself somewhere else to live. The thought of finishing the cottages didn't make her feel as happy as she imagined it would. The renovations – all the planning and organisation, dealing with tradesmen and the actual physical graft – had helped take her mind off Mark, at least some of the time.

Her mobile rang, interrupting her thoughts. It was Grazyna.

'I hope I am not disturbing you, Liz, but the police have just called. They want me to take Eryk and Lukasz to the police station. I have no idea what it is about. All I can get out of the boys is that it has something to do with you?'

'Ah.'

'Do you know what is going on?'

'I think so, yes. When are you going?'

'They want to see us straight away.'

'I'll meet you there in fifteen minutes.'

IT TOOK LONGER for her to get there. The narrow streets of the East Cliff were thick with Goth pedestrians, and when she reached the swing bridge that led over to the West Cliff, it was open and impassable. She had to wait for a yacht to pass through to the marina before it closed again and she could cross. Finally, she reached the police station, an ugly seventies building on Spring Hill.

Grazyna and the boys were in the public waiting room.

'Oh, Liz!' exclaimed Grazyna when she saw her. 'I am so glad you are here.' Her handsome face was drawn into lines of anxiety. 'I cannot get any sense out of these two at all!'

Lukasz and Eryk glared at Liz. If looks could kill, she'd be as dead as Donnie Satterthwaite. She didn't really blame them.

'Tell me, please, what all this is about!' said Grazyna.

Liz didn't know where to start. She was about to try when a door opened, and Detective Inspector Flint marched through it.

She glared at Liz. 'What are you doing here?'

Liz looked helplessly at Grazyna.

'Mrs McLuckie is my friend. I asked her to come.'

'Well, *I* didn't. She's not coming to the interview.'

'Surely the North Yorkshire police force does not discriminate against single parents? Am I not entitled to the support of a friend?'

Flint opened her mouth.

'Also my English is not perfect. You would not want me to misunderstand anything that is said, I think?'

Flint snapped her mouth shut again and turned on her heel, clearly expecting them all to follow her. Liz smothered a smile with her hand. Grazyna had an excellent command of English, but the Detective Inspector wasn't to know that. As far as brains and determination were concerned, Flint and Grazyna seemed a pretty even match. This could be interesting.

'I'M NOT interested in what you had for tea that night,' said Flint through gritted teeth. 'All I want to know is…'

'You said you wanted to know *all* the details,' said Lukasz.

'You did,' said Eryk. 'You said *all* the details.'

'That's definitely what you said.' Lukasz crossed his arms and lifted his chin.

They'd been in the interview room for more than forty minutes, and Liz doubted Flint had discovered anything she didn't already know. Grazyna had heard enough to have picked up the gist of what was going on, but hadn't had to speak in the boys' defence at all. They were doing fine on their own.

'Why pick on Mr Satterthwaite?' asked Flint. 'Why him in particular?'

'Why?' echoed Lukasz. "Cos he's a dick, that's why.'

Eryk tittered.

Constable Williams grinned too. Luckily, he was sitting slightly behind Flint, and she couldn't see him.

'He's a *dead* dick now, isn't he?' Flint snapped, clearly deciding she'd had enough. 'So let's take this seriously, shall we?'

The grins vanished.

'Say sorry to the inspector,' said Grazyna.

'Sorry.'

'Sorry.'

'Sorry,' said Constable Williams instinctively.

Flint flashed him a scowl, then turned back to the boys. 'The fact remains you broke into Mr Satterthwaite's home...'

'We didn't! We just walked in.'

Flint ignored the interruption. 'Without his permission... which is technically home invasion... and then left graffiti on his wall.'

The boys lapsed into silence.

'And then there was the howling,' said Flint. 'Where shall we start with that? Causing a disturbance? Disorderly conduct? You gave Mrs Gladwell a heart attack.'

'Actually,' cut in Liz, 'they didn't. Iris said she *saw* the Barghest.'

Flint raised an eyebrow.

Liz realised, a little late, that her interference wouldn't help the boys. She didn't think Flint was going to charge them with anything, so she should just let the DI say what she wanted to say, and then they could get out of there.

'There will be no more howling, understand? No more wasting police time. Constable Williams spent two hours at the Duke of York last night taking statements.'

Liz glanced at Williams. If he'd spent two hours in the pub, he probably wasn't just taking statements. A certain glint in his eyes when he met hers confirmed her suspicions.

'That wasn't us,' said Lukasz to Flint. 'At the Duke of York. We only howled in Neptune Yard.'

'Right.' Flint looked sceptical.

'It's true! We only howled that one time.'

Flint looked from one boy to the other. Their faces were the picture of innocence, but Liz knew that picture couldn't be trusted. Flint knew that too.

'No more howling. If I hear even so much as a whiff of a howl in this town again, I'll charge you both with disturbing the peace. Understand?'

The boys obviously didn't look as abashed as she thought they should, because she hammered her point home.

'And I'll fine your mother.'

That had the desired effect. The boys hung their heads. Grazyna's face was stony.

Flint looked thoughtfully at the boys. 'We've had some vandalism in the town lately. Window boxes smashed, fences torn down. I don't suppose either of you know anything about that?'

'I object, Inspector!' Grazyna glared at Flint. 'You cannot use this dog business as an excuse to accuse my boys of every petty crime. It is unjust.'

Flint smiled coldly at her. 'For someone with an imperfect grasp of English, Mrs Polonsky, you manage pretty well.'

WHEN THEY GOT OUTSIDE, Grazyna turned gratefully to Liz.

'Thank you for coming. I still don't understand what you had to do with all this.'

'She's a dirty snitch, that's what!'

'Lukasz! Apologise to Mrs McLuckie right now.'

'Sorry.' His face said he was anything but. His brother was also glaring at her.

'I'd better get them home,' said Grazyna. She suddenly looked very tired. 'Thank you again.'

Liz watched them go up the hill. Lukasz turned round to throw her one last dirty look. She'd like to explain to them why she'd had to tell Kevin about the paw print, but she didn't think they would understand. They'd probably never forgive her.

The rain started as she walked home, making pedestrians dash for shelter. She hadn't brought an umbrella, so resigned herself to getting wet. Cars swished past her as she headed for the harbour. When she was there, she stopped on the swing bridge to watch the rain patter on the surface of the water underneath.

She was worried for Grazyna and Gillian. Whatever they'd done to get on the list, Satterthwaite must have had concrete evidence about it. If so, where would he have kept it? There was no sign anyone had searched his cottage. Even his laptop had been untouched. If the murderer was one of his blackmail victims, wouldn't he or she have been looking for whatever proof Satterthwaite had? Liz frowned. It was all very puzzling.

She heard footsteps behind her. Liz turned to see a woman hurrying head down across the bridge through the rain, and recognised the cloche hat. Dora Spackle never even looked up at Liz, even though Liz knew she must have seen her.

'Afternoon, Dora,' she called, determined to get the woman to acknowledge her. Dora just grunted as she hurried past. Liz watched her go. She seemed to be popping up everywhere lately. Liz knew Dora had a penchant for other people's business, and for writing threatening letters. Could she have had anything to do with Satterthwaite's blackmailing scam? Liz dismissed the thought. It was unlikely.

9

It was still raining the next morning. Liz watched the rain from her kitchen window. It was falling so hard that it was bouncing at least four inches back up off the cobbles. There was no one around apart from Mike the fish-monger, dressed in his high-vis vest, hauling a tray of herring to the smokehouse next door. On impulse, she grabbed her raincoat from the hook and went out to see him.

'Morning, Mrs McLuckie!' He was surprised by her sudden appearance. 'Nice weather we're having.'

Liz laughed. 'Fancy something warm when you've dropped those off?'

'Don't mind if I do.' He pulled a face. 'I'm soaked through, though. Are you sure?'

'I'll put the kettle on.'

Mike made his delivery to the smokehouse and returned to Gull Cottage. Nelson got out of his basket and went to investigate the newcomer.

'Hullo, Nelson, old lad.' Mike bent down to ruffle the dog's ears with a big hand. 'How's things?'

'He's a bit put out. I haven't given him a proper walk yet. We just stuck our noses out for two minutes.'

'Aye, well, you really don't want to be out in this, do you?' He patted Nelson's head. 'You'd be wetter than an otter's pocket.'

He pushed his hood back and wiped rain off his red cheeks. Liz handed him his mug of tea.

'Milk, two sugars?' She hoped she'd remembered it right.

'Perfect.'

She indicated he should take a seat, but he shook his head. 'I'll just stand here if you don't mind. I don't want to get everything wet.' He sipped his tea and sighed. 'That's grand. Just what the doctor ordered.'

Mike was a good source of information in the town. If he'd been a woman, some might have called him a gossip.

'So how are things in the world of fish?' Liz sipped her own tea.

'Not too bad. The festival's keeping all the restaurants busy. And the weather's been pretty good, so the boats have been able to get out.'

'Do you supply the Crab and Cockle at all?'

'I do. I don't eat there, though. Bit pricey for me. And I like my fish plain, not messed about with.'

'Marty Davidson owns it, doesn't he?'

Mike nodded. 'The lad's a hard grafter. Went to school with one of my boys, and left with no qualifications, but worked his way up in the trade from the bottom. His heart's in the right place too. He's mentoring some of the kids from Wellworth Hall.'

Wellworth Hall was a special-needs school in York. Helping disadvantaged children didn't sound like something a murderer would do, but on the other hand, if Davidson had worked his way up from nothing, he must have found life tough. He would surely fight to protect what he'd worked for.

'Going to treat yourself, are you?' asked Mike.

Liz struggled to remember what they were talking about. The Crab and Cockle. 'Oh. Yes. Maybe when the festival's over.'

'Well, you could do worse than Marty's place.' He drained his mug and smacked his lips. 'Better get on. Fish can't deliver themselves. Thanks for the brew!'

He pulled his hood up again.

'It's still raining hard out there,' said Liz.

'Oh, don't worry about that. I can only get so wet, can't I? Besides, the sun will be out soon.'

Liz looked at him doubtfully. 'Do you think so?'

'I *know* so. It'll be cracking the cobbles by lunchtime, mark my words.'

He was right. Partly right, anyway. By midday, the sun wasn't exactly cracking the cobbles – it was October, after all – but it was making a fair effort. The rain had passed, leaving everything clean and sweet-smelling. Liz and Nelson lifted their faces to the gentle warmth as they set off through the town.

Church Street was its usual busy self, full of black-clad visitors exploring the narrow streets and their shops selling souvenirs, candy and handmade jewellery. The Jet shops were a particular favourite during the festival. Whitby Jet, a coal-black, fossilised gemstone, had been popular with the Victorians for use as mourning jewellery – a fashion set by Queen Victoria. Unsurprisingly, it was also a hit with the sombre, death-obsessed Goths.

Progress was quite slow, as every few yards or so, someone would stop to make a fuss of Nelson. For a dog that was supposedly the ugliest dog in Yorkshire, he attracted a lot of positive attention. Liz wasn't sure who'd originally given him that title, but strongly suspected Dora Spackle.

'Is he a bulldog?' A young man dressed as a plague doctor took off his mask to rub Nelson's head.

'English bull terrier.'

'Cool.'

Nelson, as impervious to compliments as he was to insults, accepted the plague doctor's homage until they walked on again. Liz was relieved when they got out of the narrow streets and into the main thoroughfare of the town, where they were able to walk faster and steer clear of admirers.

They were heading for a part of town Liz rarely visited, the amusement arcades by the harbour. They turned right on the other side of the swing bridge and made their way down St Ann's Staith, a narrow pedestrian thoroughfare, with shops on one side and the sea on the other. This was where the hardcore tourist shops could be found, their facades festooned with racks of postcards, plastic buckets and spades, inflatable dolphins and killer whales. There were ice-cream shops too, selling ices and bags of candy floss. The aroma of spun sugar mingled with the smell of the sea and fish. Farther down, the pedestrian area rejoined the road, giving way to pubs, seafood shacks, hot-dog stalls, and the low, red-brick building of Whitby fish market, shutters down at that time of the day.

At last, Liz and Nelson arrived at the open frontages of the amusement arcades. It was an assault on the senses, with the whirr and clang of slot machines and flashing lights. 'Amuse-ments!' bellowed the signage. 'Fun!' 'Family Entertainment!' The largest of the arcades was Penny City, with an impressive dark blue facade, striped with pink neon. Liz was pretty sure it was owned by Philip Nethergate.

She hesitated outside. While the arcades were very busy in the summer, in autumn, there weren't many people playing the machines, like today. Liz supposed that Goths generally pursued different pleasures. Nelson gave her a look, as if to say 'Really? We're going in *there*?'

She realised too late that she probably shouldn't have brought him. Were dogs even allowed? She couldn't see any signs that said otherwise, so they went in.

Inside, the noise was even more alarming. She supposed the machines made noises even when there was no one playing them. That made sense. A silent arcade wasn't likely to tempt anyone in off the street. She could see all the usual machines she remembered from her childhood – penny waterfalls, claw grabbers and slot machines – but also a lot she didn't know. Video games, mostly – shoot-'em-ups, as well as superhero games and Formula 1 simulators. She only had a five-pound note in her pocket, so looked around for the cashier's kiosk. She spotted a sign that shrieked 'Cash!' near the back of the arcade, and headed towards it. There was a face she knew inside the glass box.

'Hello!'

'Mrs McLuckie! What are you doing in here?' Fiona Mellor's broad face broke into a smile that showed her metal braces.

'I could ask you the same thing.' Fiona was usually to be found in the abbey gift shop.

Fiona shrugged. 'Oh, you know, every little helps. I have three part-time jobs.'

'Good for you.' Liz didn't understand why everyone insisted that young people were lazy. All the ones she knew were very hard working.

'I wouldn't think slot machines were your thing,' said Fiona.

'I like to try my luck –' Liz presented her five-pound note '– just in case Fortune decides to smile on me.'

Fiona gave her an ironic look. It was hardly likely to happen there.

'How do you want it?'

'One pound in twos, and the rest in tens, please.'

'Are you sure? Most of the games take twenty-pence pieces.'

Liz's eyebrows rose. So much for Penny City.

'Twenties not tens, then.' She watched Fiona count out the money. 'Philip Nethergate owns this arcade, doesn't he?'

'Yeah.' Fiona gave her the coins.

'What's he like to work for?'

'Oh, you know, not too bad.' Fiona's gaze slid past Liz. Liz looked over her shoulder. There was a man leaning in the shadows behind her, that she hadn't noticed when she'd approached the kiosk. He was wearing a black leather jacket and was watching them.

She didn't let that put her off. She'd come here to find out more about Nethergate, and Fiona was the perfect opportunity. 'He owns quite a few businesses in the town, doesn't he?'

'I think so.'

'The garage on Spital Bridge? And the crazy golf on the West Cliff?'

'Mmm. I think so.'

Liz had thought that was the case, but hadn't been able to verify it online. Details of Nethergate's business enterprises had been strangely opaque. 'Do you know if he...'

'You can't bring that dog in here.' The voice was loud in Liz's ear and made her jump. The man in the shadows looked bigger now that he was standing beside her. Much bigger. He was close enough for her to see the stubble on his chin and a scar that ran from his left ear to his mouth.

'Sorry, I didn't see any signs.'

'No dogs.'

'But I've just got my change. I want to spend it.'

'No dogs.'

Liz knew she was beaten. Tying Nelson up outside wasn't

an option.

'Let me change that back for you.' Fiona took Liz's coins and swapped them for the five-pound note again.

'Thank you.'

Fiona gave her an embarrassed smile, and Liz retreated with Nelson. She felt the man's eyes on her all the way back onto the pavement.

She took a lungful of fresh, fishy air. She knew from her research that the scarred man wasn't the owner. The images she'd found on the internet showed Philip Nethergate was a smooth-looking man who favoured tailored suits. He probably wouldn't be caught dead in a leather jacket or needing a shave. Whoever the scarred man was, she was pretty sure he hadn't thrown her out of the arcade because of Nelson.

'Come on,' she said to Nelson, 'let's get some lunch.'

They headed away from the arcades, back towards the East Cliff and home.

They were waiting at the bridge for a boat to pass, when a creeping sensation of uneasiness came over Liz. She turned and scanned the crowd. A jolt of electricity ran through her. The man with the leather jacket was leaning on the harbour railing, not thirty feet away. He was looking at the water, but Liz wasn't fooled. She'd already felt the weight of his gaze. The bridge bell clanged, the barrier went up, and the waiting crowd surged forward to cross.

'Go, Nelson!' They practically galloped over the bridge.

When they reached the other side, Liz risked another glance over her shoulder. The man had also picked up speed and was hurrying after them.

Damn. Liz took the first left down Sandgate and put on an extra burst of speed while her pursuer couldn't see her. They'd almost reached the Full Moon café when he appeared at the end of the street. He spotted them through the crowd and followed.

They ducked into the café. It was full of customers, with only Grazyna serving.

'Sorry, Liz,' she said with a grimace. 'There is no table for you.'

'No worries,' gasped Liz. 'We're just passing through.' She put her finger to her lips and headed for the beaded curtain. They went through into the corridor and then into the kitchen. The air was thick with steam and the aroma of garlic.

Mags' eyes opened wide when she saw Liz and Nelson. Liz didn't break stride.

'Sorry, not stopping. If anyone asks, you haven't seen us.'

Leaving Mags open-mouthed, they dashed out the back door and into the alley behind the café. It led down to the shore.

Liz hurried Nelson along the beach. He was enjoying himself immensely, wearing a huge grin as they sped over the pebbles. At the lifeboat station, Liz looked behind them again. The beach was deserted, so she guided Nelson up, into the narrow tunnel of New Way Ghaut that led back to Church Street, the Duke of York, Henrietta Street and safety.

It was only when she'd closed the door of Gull Cottage behind them that she allowed herself a sigh of relief. But she was still worried. Fiona didn't know exactly where she lived, but knew her name. The scarred man only had to ask. As the only McLuckie in Whitby's phone book, she wouldn't be hard to find.

It was pretty safe to assume the scarred man worked for Nethergate and didn't like people asking questions about his boss. That would certainly make sense if Nethergate was being blackmailed. Was the scarred man just following her, or did he have something more sinister in mind?

She had no idea, but she did know one thing: Philip Nethergate was a man with secrets.

10

L iz peered at her reflection in the spotted glass of the bathroom mirror and was surprised to find she was quite happy with it. In spite of her frantic flight along the beach earlier, she was having a good hair day. Now she had it pinned on top of her head, with a few loose tendrils falling around her face. Her chestnut colouring went well with the midnight-blue jersey dress she'd chosen, and with the sapphires that dangled from her ears. The earrings had been a present from Mark for their tenth anniversary and had been ridiculously expensive. She only wore them on special occasions.

Tonight, she wanted to look her best, because Benedict had invited her to a party at the Captain Cook museum. An ex-Navy man and expert on maritime antiques, he'd recently been appointed to the board of trustees.

She smiled at her reflection. The bathroom lighting was kind, hiding the lines she knew were there, under her make-up. It still took her by surprise sometimes when she caught sight of herself in a mirror, and instead of the twenty-something girl she expected, she would see a fifty-something woman staring back at her. She supposed that was the same for everyone. On the whole, however, she thought she didn't look too bad for her age and was happy with her appearance. Age had added a certain depth to it, a certain self-assurance that no amount of make-up or youthful bravado could supply.

HER CONFIDENCE WOBBLED A LITTLE, forty minutes later, when she saw how busy it was in the museum. The great and the good of the town – sixty or so people – were crammed into the low-ceilinged main exhibition space on the first floor. It was a narrow, four-storey building, criss-crossed with wooden beams and filled with seafaring exhibits.

She took a glass of wine from one of the servers and sipped it, trying not to fidget. Even though she wasn't particularly comfortable in high heels, she was glad she'd decided to wear them, and pleased she'd made an effort with her appearance.

Everyone looked very glamorous. The men were all wearing shirts and ties, and the women sparkled in evening dresses and jewellery. She wondered what Tilly and Mags would be wearing when they turned up. She knew they'd also been invited by Benedict, but for some reason they hadn't yet put in an appearance.

Liz continued to sip her wine, trying not to feel like a spare part. She could see Benedict across the room, talking to another man, one arm around Gillian's waist. Gillian looked sensational in a figure-hugging black dress, her short hair slicked behind her ears in a style that suited her elfin features. Far too sexy for a woman of the cloth, decided Liz with a sniff. And for a woman in her forties.

She wished she hadn't come. Perhaps she could just sneak away?

Before she could put any plan in motion, Benedict spotted her and waved her over.

'Liz! I didn't see you there. Come and meet Councillor Johnson.'

The councillor smiled. 'Charlie, please.'

Charlie Johnson. Wasn't he on Satterthwaite's list?

As Liz reached the little group, the councillor held out his hand to her. He was a substantial man with piercing blue eyes and a knowing air. 'It's Mrs McLuckie, isn't it? I've been wanting to meet you. Weren't you the heroine of our little crime drama in the summer?'

'She was,' said Benedict. 'She was very brave.'

Liz blushed.

The councillor took her hand and, to her horror, brought it to his lips.

'Charmed.' His eyes burned into hers. Liz slid her gaze away, panicked, and met Benedict's cool grey one. He frowned.

'You must let me take you to dinner some time,' said Johnson, 'so you can tell me all about it.'

Liz couldn't think of a response, so she just laughed. It sounded a little strained.

Gillian grinned. 'Make sure you don't leave out the bit about the fish. That's my favourite part.'

'I don't remember hearing anything about a fish,' said Johnson. He still had hold of Liz's hand, but she managed to prise it loose.

'There's nothing really to tell.' She resisted the urge to wipe her hand on her dress.

'Reverend! Do you have a minute?' Two elderly ladies were waving at Gillian from the other side of the room. Gillian excused herself and went to join them.

Benedict smiled coldly at the councillor. 'I don't think I've seen you at any of our events before.'

Johnson ignored him. 'I really must show you the new knot exhibit, Liz.' He turned back to Benedict. 'You don't mind if I steal her from you?'

'Of course not.'

Liz stared at Benedict. Had she imagined it, or had the left side of his mouth just twitched? Benedict had a tell that she'd come to recognise during their many evenings playing mahjong. Whenever he bluffed or told a lie, the left-hand corner of his mouth would twitch. It was a dead giveaway, and one he was entirely unable to control, even though she'd warned him about it. She was sure it *had* just given him away, but didn't dare speculate what that might mean.

She didn't have time to think too hard about it, because before she knew it, she was being towed towards the farthest corner of the room. The farthest *darkest* corner. *Dear God.*

They reached the knot display, an alcove with a couple of dozen rope knots displayed in it: anchor hitch, cleat hitch, bowline, buntline, etc. It wasn't a new display, or a particularly interesting one, although Liz would never have said so to Benedict, who had a thing for knots. Johnson clearly didn't. He didn't even glance at the exhibits, but fixed her with a speculative stare.

'I saw your photograph in the *Bugle*,' he said, 'but I had no idea you were so different, so gorgeous in the flesh.'

Liz pulled her hand away. Did he think that was a compliment?

'I think we should go back to the others,' she said. But he grabbed her hand again.

'I wish there was a bit more privacy in here. I want to get to know you better.'

'Can I have a word, Councillor?'

Liz never thought she'd be grateful to see Dora Spackle. The curator of the abbey museum had apparently sprung from nowhere, like a tweed-clad fairy, but of course, it was entirely natural she'd be invited.

'I'd like to talk to you about the recycling collection up at the abbey.' Dora glanced at Liz and Johnson's conjoined hands and sniffed.

'Can't it wait, Mrs Spackle?' Johnson tried and failed to keep exasperation from his voice. Liz freed her hand.

'Miss.'

'*Miss* Spackle, as you see, I'm showing Mrs McLuckie –'

'Recycling is important,' Dora insisted.

'Of course it is, but –'

'My question is, should our plastic sheeting be boxed with the plastics or nonrecyclables?'

'I really couldn't tell you. I don't have anything to do with waste –'

'Global warming is a serious issue.'

'Indeed it is, but –'

'Excuse me.' Liz saw her chance and fled.

She didn't stop to say goodbye to Benedict and Gillian, but went straight downstairs to the cloakroom, grabbed her coat, and ran into the night. She was furious! A man like that, a man in power – even if it was just petty provincial power – thinking he had the right to grab her? God knew how many other women he'd molested. She should have told him to get knotted. Or kneed him in the double hitch.

If she was honest, she was disappointed in Benedict too. He'd allowed her to be dragged away by that awful man. He clearly didn't care about her at all, whatever that stupid twitch of his might have meant. As she stomped along the cobbles of Church Street, she went over on her ankle.

'Damn it!'

She'd forgotten about her heels. She took them off and continued to stomp. Church Street was still quite hectic, with pub-going Goths dressed in their most outrageous costumes. No one looked twice at her bare feet.

By the time she reached the bottom of the abbey steps, her temper had cooled, and so had her toes. In fact, they were completely numb. She hobbled down Henrietta Street, and as she got closer to Gull Cottage, she could see someone sitting on the doorstep. Fear flashed through her. Had the scarred man discovered where she lived? Then she heaved a sigh of relief – the figure was far too small.

It was Tilly. When her friend lifted her head, Liz could see her cheeks were streaked with mascara.

'Liz! I'm so glad you're home.'

'What's the matter?'

'I can't tell you out here. Can I come in?'

Liz let them into the cottage, ignoring a bouncing Nelson, who was delighted to see them both. She sat Tilly on one of the kitchen chairs. She was frozen.

'How long have you been out there?'

Tilly shrugged. 'I'd forgotten you were at the museum.'

Liz crouched to light the old gas fire. It took several attempts, but eventually it spluttered into life. She put the kettle on the stove.

'Try to warm yourself up. I won't be a minute.'

She ran upstairs and found a pair of socks in her bedroom. She pulled them quickly over her dirty feet and grabbed a blanket. When she got back downstairs, she draped the blanket over Tilly's shoulders.

'Better?'

Tilly nodded. 'Yes, thanks. I hadn't realised how cold it was out there.'

'What's going on?'

'Mags has thrown me out.'

Liz's eyes widened.

'And I totally deserve it.' Tilly's words caught on a sob.

Liz stared at her. 'Do you want to tell me about it?' she asked.

What could have made the usually mild-mannered Mags lose her temper? It had to be something massive. Had Tilly turned to burglary again? Had she been unfaithful?

'It's the drinks licence.'

Liz frowned.

Tilly wiped her nose with the back of her hand. 'When we were turned down, I went to see someone at the council, and I begged him. He said there was nothing he could do, unless...' Tilly tailed off and looked at Liz with beseeching eyes.

'Unless you paid him?'

Tilly nodded miserably. 'I was an idiot. I took the money from our savings. I was going to put it back – and more – as soon as we'd made some money on the drink sales. But Mags saw the balance today. I had to tell her what I'd done. She went nuts.'

Ouch.

'She's terrified we'll get into trouble. Says she's not going to prison again, even for me.'

Liz had been shocked when she'd first discovered Tilly and Mags had met in a young offenders' institution. Tilly had been there for breaking and entering, and Mags for some undisclosed offence. Shortly after they'd got out, Mags had inherited a sizeable amount of money from her aunt, and after travelling the world together, the pair had settled down and bought the café. They worked hard and were on the straight and narrow. Or straightish and narrow, as far as Tilly was concerned. Liz knew from their adventures in the summer that Tilly had occasionally strayed a tiny bit, but nothing serious, and certainly nothing anywhere near as bad as bribing a councillor. Mags was right to be furious.

The kettle whistled on the stove. Tilly stared into the gas fire, and Liz went to make cocoa. As Liz got the milk from the fridge, a thought occurred to her.

'This councillor you bribed,' she asked. 'It wasn't Charlie Johnson, by any chance?'

11

L iz stared at the card in her hand.

Dearest Liz – Such a pleasure to meet you last night.
Please let me take you to dinner. Call me? Charlie.

HE'D WRITTEN his mobile number on the bottom. Liz crumpled it up and threw it in the bin. It had arrived with three dozen white roses that were now dotted around the kitchen in several vases. Liz couldn't bring herself to throw them away as well – they were too lovely, and it wasn't their fault they'd been sent by a handsy, criminally fraudulent fool.

She was now in a tricky situation. What she really wanted to do was ram Councillor Charlie Johnson's dinner invitation where the sun didn't shine, but she couldn't afford to make an enemy of him, for Tilly's sake. Although she'd been surprised by Tilly's rash behaviour, she hadn't been in the least bit surprised to discover it was Johnson who'd taken the bribe.

Had Satterthwaite found out about his illegal activities? Was that why he was blackmailing him? Could Johnson be the poisoner? Liz wouldn't put it past him.

Niall stumbled into the kitchen, wearing his Barghest T-shirt, rubbing sleep from his eyes. 'Is there someone upstairs?' he asked. 'Do we have a ghost, or did you pull last night?'

'Very funny.' Liz didn't think it was funny at all. 'It's Tilly.'

'What?'

'Mags has thrown her out.'

'*What?*'

'Long story.'

He looked around the room. 'What's with all the flowers?' Then he grinned. 'You *did* pull last night!'

'Shut up and make yourself some breakfast. There's croissants if you want them.'

She took a rose from one of the vases, laid it in Neville and Jackie's breakfast basket, and took the basket next door. When she got back, Tilly was also up, sitting forlornly at the kitchen table.

'I didn't sleep a wink last night,' she said.

That wasn't news to Liz. She'd had to lie beside her in the double bed, listening to her sigh and thrash around.

'You have to talk to Mags today,' said Liz. 'Explain.'

'Explain? There is no explanation, apart from me being stupid.'

'Then say that. And grovel. Grovel a lot.'

Niall had been listening. 'You could take her some flowers,' he suggested. 'Liz has plenty.'

An hour later, after Tilly had showered and dressed, they pushed her out the door with an armful of roses.

'What if she won't accept my apology?' she fretted. 'I don't know if I can do this. Perhaps I should wait until she's cooled down a bit?'

'She's had all night to do that,' said Liz. 'Arguments have a habit of setting if you leave them too long.'

'Like concrete,' agreed Niall.

'You're right.' Tilly nodded. 'You're right. Here I go.'

She went. Liz hadn't even closed the door when she was back again. She thrust the roses at Liz.

'I feel stupid with these. She'll know I haven't bought them.' Then she was gone again.

'Phew,' said Liz, putting the roses back in their vase. It was far too much drama for so early in the morning.

'What'd she do, anyway?' asked Niall. 'It's not like Mags to blow up over nothing.'

'It wasn't nothing,' said Liz. 'But that's all I'm going to say.'

'Fair enough.' He saw the clock on the wall and gave a start. 'Jaysus, is that the time? I'd better get going.'

'What's the hurry?'

'The Duke's got a big do at lunchtime. Donnie Satterthwaite's memorial service.'

'Memorial service?' echoed Liz. 'That's quick, isn't it?'

'Apparently the coroner won't be releasing his body for weeks yet.' Niall gulped down the last of his croissant. 'So his ma's decided to have a service now.'

'Up at St Mary's?'

Niall nodded. 'At eleven.'

THE SQUAT EXTERIOR of St Mary's, the twelfth-century church on Whitby's East Cliff, gave no clue to its decorative interior. It had been refitted in the eighteen hundreds, with polished wooden box pews and white-painted balconies supported by barley-twist posts. It had an unusual double pulpit, with a carved canopy, and a beautiful stained-glass window over the altar that bled jewelled colours over the people gathered inside.

The clock in the tower struck eleven, and the memorial service started, led by Gillian, who was looking a lot less glamorous in her clerical collar than she had in her black dress the night before. Liz, sitting at the back, only listened with half an ear, more interested in Danny Satterthwaite's mourners than she was in the service itself.

Satterthwaite's mother – Liz assumed it was his mother – sat in the front pew, an elegant woman with an upswept grey chignon, wearing an expensive-looking grey skirt suit and grey leather gloves. It was hard to tell how old she was, but Liz guessed she was somewhere in her late sixties or early seventies. On either side of Satterthwaite's mother sat Emma Summers and Dora Spackle. Liz was surprised to see Dora there. She didn't think Dora had many friends.

Liz speculated. If Satterthwaite was blackmailing his list of people, he must have had a cache of evidence against them. Police had found nothing at his cottage, so where had he kept it? At his mum's house? Was the old lady in danger?

Just as the possibility occurred to her, Liz spotted another two familiar figures. Kevin and DI Flint were sitting at the end of one of the pews, about halfway down the church. She sank a little lower into her own seat, hoping they hadn't seen her.

The service continued. Gillian was followed by Satterthwaite's boss, the editor of the *Whitby Bugle,* who said lots of nice things about his employee's diligence and his nose for a story. After that came several of Satterthwaite's colleagues, who paid a more lukewarm tribute to their 'friend'. Satterthwaite's mother sat through it all, dabbing her eyes with a handkerchief, consoled silently by Dora and Emma Summers. Liz felt a pang of sympathy – it must be the hardest thing in the world to lose a child, at any age. She had no children, herself. Mark had had a particularly nasty bout of mumps when he was fourteen, and it had made him infertile. They'd talked about adopting, but eventually decided not to. They'd had each other, and that had been enough.

Liz felt her own eyes prickle, and blinked back the tears. She was being ridiculous.

The service ended. Liz hung around at the back, not wanting to get into conversation with anyone. She waited until the church had emptied before making her way to the front, where she stood and gazed at the stained-glass window for a minute or two, marvelling at the workmanship.

'Thank heavens that's over,' said a voice behind her. 'I really wasn't looking forward to it.'

'You did very well,' said Liz.

Gillian pulled a face. 'It was a bit tricky. I didn't really know Donnie at all. He wasn't a churchgoer, like his mum.'

Liz gave her a searching look. She obviously had no idea it was Satterthwaite who'd been blackmailing her. There were lines of weariness and tension on Gillian's face that hadn't been there in the summer. Liz felt a stab of guilt. She'd been avoiding Gillian ever since she and Benedict had started going out together, but perhaps she shouldn't have. Perhaps Gillian had needed a friend?

'How are you?' Liz asked. 'Are you okay?'

'Me?' Gillian gave a weary smile. 'I'm fine. Just tired. I might have had one too many glasses of wine at the museum last night. Where did you get to, by the way?'

Liz shrugged. 'I just decided to go home.'

'Very wise. Come on, let's get out of here. I have to get this place locked up before I go down to the Duke of York. Oh... what's this?'

Gillian had spotted something lying on the front pew. She picked it up. A grey leather glove.

'It must be Peggy's,' she said.

'Satterthwaite's mum?'

Gillian nodded. 'I doubt she'll be at the Duke of York, but I suppose I can give it to her on Sunday.'

Liz saw her opportunity. 'She might need it before then. I'll take it to her if you like.'

PEGGY SATTERTHWAITE LIVED IN A HANDSOME, four-storey Georgian house quite close to Benedict's house at Pannet Park. Like Benedict's house, and unlike many of its neighbours, it hadn't yet been divided into flats. Positioned on the edge of the park, it also had a lovely leafy view. As Liz climbed the steps to the front door, she speculated that it must be worth a fair amount of money. Donnie Satterthwaite hadn't seemed particularly well off, but she supposed that had no bearing on his mother's circumstances.

She rang the doorbell and waited. After a while, she saw movement through the frosted-glass panels, and the door opened. To Liz's surprise it was Emma Summers who opened it, wearing the dress she'd worn earlier to the memorial service.

'Hello?' said Emma.

'Hi. My name's –'

'Kathleen,' cut in Emma.

Liz frowned.

'That was what you asked me to write on your book, wasn't it?' said Emma. 'At the signing?'

'You have a good memory. Actually, that was for a friend. I'm Liz. Liz McLuckie. Is it possible to see Mrs Satterthwaite?'

Emma looked doubtful.

'Who is it, Emma?' called a voice from inside the house.

'A lady called Liz McLuckie,' Emma called back.

There was a stir, and then another voice cut in. 'Let me handle this.'

Liz's heart sank. After a moment, Dora Spackle appeared at Emma's shoulder. 'What do you want?'

'I have Mrs Satterthwaite's glove. I wanted to return it.'

Dora held out her hand. 'Give it to me. Peggy doesn't want to be disturbed just now.'

Realising she had no choice but to hand it over, Liz opened her bag to take out the glove.

'Oh, is that mine?' Peggy appeared behind her two gate-keepers. Close up, Liz could see her eyes were a startling, periwinkle blue. 'How lovely.' She took the glove from Liz. 'Where did you find it?'

'In St Mary's.'

'Silly me. But how thoughtful of you to return it. Do come in.'

'If you're sure?' Liz couldn't help but notice Dora was glowering at her.

'Of course. We're just having tea. Let me take your coat.' Peggy waved Liz inside. 'Dora, be a darling and find an extra cup for Liz.'

The sitting room was one of the loveliest rooms Liz had ever been in, with its walls painted sunshine yellow and hung with old paintings. Huge Georgian windows let in the afternoon light that reflected off a crystal chandelier and the mirror over the fireplace. Comfort hadn't been sacrificed for style, however – the chairs and sofa were super-squashy, and there was a cheerful fire burning in the grate. There was a tea tray on the coffee table with a willow-pattern teapot and three cups.

'Please make yourself at home.' Peggy's silver hair was loose on her shoulders, and she was dressed in a pink wrap-around cardigan and casual trousers. She frowned at the glove in her hand. 'I can't believe I left this. I must be getting dotty in my old age.'

'Don't be silly,' said Emma, who had settled herself in one of the armchairs.

'Yesterday I went to the post office, and when I got to the front of the queue, I realised I'd completely forgotten why I was there.' Peggy shook her head in disbelief.

'Grief can do that,' said Liz, then realised what she'd said. 'I'm so sorry for your loss, Mrs Satterthwaite. It must be very hard.'

'Thank you.' Peggy blinked back sudden tears. 'It has been rather difficult.'

'What she needs is peace and quiet,' muttered Dora, who'd appeared with an extra cup and saucer. 'Not complete strangers popping in on a whim.'

Peggy frowned at her. Liz said nothing.

Dora had a point. She'd returned the glove to satisfy her own curiosity, and because she was worried Peggy might be in danger from whoever had killed her son. But it seemed she was well guarded. Peggy poured the tea and handed her a cup.

'I don't think I saw you at the memorial service?' she said.

'I was right at the back.'

'Did you know Donnie well?'

Liz had to think quickly. 'Not really. Just through the newspaper. The service was very moving.'

'It was, wasn't it? Of course, it's not the same as a proper funeral, but...' She blinked. 'But...'

'It was a credit to him,' said Emma, 'and to you, Peggy.' She looked at Liz and Dora for support. 'Wasn't it?'

They nodded.

Peggy Satterthwaite gazed into space and frowned, as if she was trying to remember something important. Liz sipped her tea as fast as she could without appearing rude. She was deeply uncomfortable and a little ashamed of herself for being there. The glowering looks Dora kept darting at her weren't making her feel any better.

'I hope you didn't have to come too far out of your way to return the glove,' said Emma, trying gamely to resurrect the conversation.

'No,' said Liz. 'I live on the East Cliff. Henrietta Street.'

'Oh, how lovely. Such a pretty street, isn't it, Dora?'

'Hmm.' Dora slurped her tea and glared over her teacup at Liz. She was quite an odd companion for her two genteel friends.

'I live out towards Ruswarp myself,' said Emma, with an air of desperation. 'Nice and quiet.'

They lapsed into silence again.

'But not so convenient,' added Emma. 'For shops and things.'

Liz nodded. Emma was much sweeter and more gauche than Liz had expected for someone with such a high-profile career. Liz had known a few actresses over the years, and without exception, they had all been as mad as a box of frogs. Emma, on the other hand, seemed to have her head screwed on. It was quite horrifying that the son of one of her best friends had been blackmailing her. Liz wondered what she'd done to make her such a target, but then realised that most people had things in their past they weren't proud of.

She gulped the rest of her tea. 'That was lovely, thank you.' She stood up. 'I have to be going.'

Peggy returned from wherever she had drifted off to. 'So soon?'

'I need to get back to my dog. I don't like to leave him on his own for too long.'

Dora's lip curled at the mention of Nelson. 'I'll see you out.'

'Thank you again,' Peggy called after her, 'for returning my glove.'

In the hall, Dora opened the front door for Liz to leave.

'I wanted to say thank you,' said Liz, 'for saving me last night.'

'Saving you?'

'From Councillor Johnson.'

Dora looked at her blankly. Liz sighed. She'd thought that Dora's intervention the previous night might have been in the spirit of sisterhood, but she'd clearly been mistaken.

'It's not important,' said Liz.

'No.' Dora sniffed. 'I dare say it isn't.'

12

That evening the *Bugle* ran a discreet piece about the memorial service. It was separate to another, larger article about the murder and the lack of police progress. Liz suspected that Kevin had been avoiding her. Either he was nervous he might inadvertently let something slip about the investigation or that she would grill him about it. Although she missed him popping in for tea, it was actually something of a relief. The more time went on, the guiltier she felt about keeping the information about the blackmail to herself. She knew she was going to have to tell him about it soon.

She was about to put the newspaper down, when she spotted another article – *Award-winning Whitby restaurant closes.* It was about the Crab and Cockle. Marty Davidson had announced that the restaurant was shutting down, and had refused to say whether it was permanent or temporary. Liz frowned. She still had Davidson in her sights as the mysterious MD on Satterthwaite's calendar. It was odd that he'd chosen to close his restaurant right in the middle of the Goth Festival, when he would be making money. Why had he decided to do that? She had no idea, but she knew someone who might.

THE NEXT MORNING, she took Nelson for his walk as soon as the sun rose over the East Cliff, and then positioned herself at the kitchen window for Mike to make an appearance. She waited and waited, but by the time nine o'clock came around, she realised the smokehouse wasn't getting a delivery that morning.

So, after dropping Neville and Jackie's breakfast basket at Kipper Cottage, she set off into the town. It was another pleasant day, and the streets of the old town were already busy, with a mix of locals and Goths. Quite a few of the black-clad visitors looked a little worse for wear from the night before. There were only three days of the festival left, so she supposed they were making the most of it.

She crossed the swing bridge and made her way to Baxtergate, one of the main shopping streets of the West Cliff. Although the buildings were still historical – Victorian mostly – there was a more contemporary mix of shops, the kinds of chain stores you would see in any northern town, interspersed with banks and estate agents. One of the few independent shops among them was Howson's the fishmonger. Howson's was something of a Whitby institution, smartly painted in green, with its original Victorian tiles showing pictorial scenes of the sea and fish. It had an impressive display arranged on ice in the window – a shoal of silver-striped mackerel, piles of freshly shelled scallops, sides of salmon, and huge, gaping cod. Liz stuck her head inside the shop. Although there was quite a queue at the counter, there was no sign of Mike. She caught the eye of one of the women serving, an older woman with a no-nonsense air. Liz wondered if she was his wife.

'I'm looking for Mike?' she called out to her.

'Out back. In the yard.'

Liz nodded her thanks.

'He's not in a good mood, mind.'

As Liz retraced her steps along Baxtergate and into the lane that ran behind it, she wondered what had upset Mike. She'd never seen him anything other than upbeat. Turning down the lane, she spotted his van parked beside a pile of wood. The gate to his yard was open. As she approached the gate, a plank of wood came flying out and landed with a crash on top of the pile.

'Hello!' she called, not wanting to be beheaded by another wooden missile. She poked her head into the yard.

'Mrs Mac,' said Mike, his eyes widening in surprise.

His yard was littered with broken pieces of wood. Smashed crates, Liz guessed. Although there were a few plastic trays stacked in the corner, Mike preferred the traditional, wooden ones. But there weren't many left. Most were lying broken on the cobbles.

'What happened here?' she asked.

Mike scowled. 'Ruddy kids.'

'Really?'

'I'm betting it's them Polonsky twins. I've chased them off more than once.'

'I don't think Eryk and Lukasz would do this.' But even as she said it, she wasn't completely sure. It might be something the boys would do out of mischief, without realising they were potentially affecting someone's livelihood.

'Know them, do you?' asked Mike, grim-faced. Liz nodded. 'If you know their mother too, you might want to tell her to keep a better eye on them. I've seen them out and about all hours, even when they should be at school.'

Liz hoped he was mistaken. If the boys were truanting,

that was something else poor Grazyna would have to deal with.

Mike straightened up. 'Were you looking for me, Mrs Mac?'

'Oh, yes.' Liz decided just to plunge in. 'I wondered if you knew anything about the Crab and Cockle closing down.'

Mike lifted his eyebrows and tutted. 'Bad business.'

'Bad? How?'

He eyed her guiltily. 'By rights, I shouldn't say anything.'

'Why not?'

'Marty doesn't want it getting out.'

Liz waited for more.

'Rats,' he said eventually.

'Rats?'

'Dozens of them. He's shut the place down before the public health gets wind of it. That way he can open again, no questions asked, when he manages to get rid.'

'Where did they come from?'

'That's the mystery, isn't it? There was no sign of them on Wednesday, and then yesterday the place was overrun. He's trying to clear them out on the quiet, with poison and suchlike.'

Poison. Does rat poison contain strychnine? Liz dismissed the thought. It was a tenuous link.

'How long's that going to take?' she asked.

'Who knows? The lad's at his wit's end.'

'Strange for them to suddenly appear like that.'

Mike didn't meet her eyes, but shrugged, and bent to pick up another armful of wood. His silence was eloquent.

'You think someone *put* the rats there?'

Mike still said nothing, but made a show of huffing and puffing across the yard before tossing the wood into the lane.

'Mike, is there someone with a vendetta against Marty Davidson?'

The fishmonger sighed and straightened up again. 'I've already said too much.' He hesitated. 'Vendetta might be too strong a word, Mrs Mac, but yes, there is someone who'd like to see him go out of business.'

'Who?'

Mike shook his head. His usually red cheeks were pale, and his mouth was set into a grim line. She realised she was going to get nothing more from him on the matter.

'Do you need a hand with this lot?' She eyed the wood without enthusiasm. She didn't particularly want to get her hands dirty, but felt she should offer.

To her surprise, Mike laughed. 'Get on with you! I've got two gurty, great lads lounging around in the house somewhere. If I want help, I'll get them layabouts to do it.' He chuckled. 'Thanks for asking, though.'

Liz nodded and left him chortling, more like his usual self. She couldn't imagine why the idea of her helping him with the wood had been so funny.

As she headed back through town, she thought about what he'd told her. Had someone put rats in the Crab and Cockle? How would someone even get hold of so many? Buy them in a pet shop? The idea seemed far-fetched, but Mike clearly believed there was more to the situation than an innocent pest invasion. It was certainly something to think about.

Liz looked up and realised with surprise that she'd already reached the pedestrian crossing on New Quay. It was a busy stretch of road, and the lights usually took a while to change. She waited at the edge of the kerb with the other pedestrians and continued to mull things over. Why would someone want Marty Davidson to go out of business?

A thought occurred. The Crab and Cockle must have a drinks licence, so they could sell alcohol with their food. But that kind of licence usually had a cut-off point of 11 pm. Had Marty Davidson maybe applied for an extended licence so he could serve alcohol later, through the festival? Did he know Charlie Johnson? Had Johnson demanded a bribe? Had Davidson refused?

Someone shoved her suddenly between the shoulder blades. She stumbled out into the road. A blue van hurtled towards her. She saw the driver's shocked face through the windscreen and heard the screech of tyres.

Then everything went black.

13

'You're a very lucky woman, Mrs McLuckie.' The young nurse dabbed at the cut on Liz's forehead, making her wince. 'If Miss Spackle hadn't pulled you out of the way in time, who knows what might have happened.'

'Spackle?' echoed Liz. Her head ached; she was having trouble stringing her thoughts together.

'Dora Spackle.' The nurse nodded. 'She's getting her wrist strapped in the next cubicle. The pair of you hit the ground pretty hard.'

Great, thought Liz. *Now I owe Dora Spackle my life.* What was with the woman anyway, popping up all the time? What was she? A ruddy genie?

'You're going to have to take it easy with that concussion. We should probably keep you in overnight, just in case.'

'No.' Liz shook her head. It made her brain hurt. 'Nelson needs me.'

The nurse looked at her oddly.

'My dog,' said Liz.

The nurse grinned. 'Ah. That's a relief. I thought you were

proper away with the fairies there. Well, you could always ask someone else to look after him, couldn't you? Let's see what the doctor says. She shouldn't be too long.' She picked up the bloody, cotton wool and left the cubicle.

Liz let herself sink back onto the bed and closed her eyes. She tried to piece together what had happened. She'd been standing at the crossing... thinking about rats... and... someone had pushed her! She sat up quickly, then sank back down with a groan. She closed her eyes again. Someone had definitely pushed her into the road.

'Are you awake?'

Liz opened her eyes to see Dora peering down at her. Her cloche hat was slightly awry, and she had her left arm in a sling, but otherwise she looked her usual, irritable self.

Liz sat up with a wince. 'How's your wrist?'

'Could be worse. It's just a sprain.'

'Thank you for pulling me out of the road.'

Dora sniffed. 'I'd have done it for anyone.'

'You must have been right behind me,' said Liz.

Dora looked at her suspiciously. 'I suppose.'

'Did you see who pushed me?'

'Pushed you?'

'Into the road.'

'No one pushed you. You just fell off the kerb.'

'Are you sure?'

Dora frowned at her. 'Concussions can be dangerous, can't they? Make you go loopy.'

'I'm not loopy.'

'No loopier than usual, I suppose.'

'What's that supposed to mean?'

'Well, you have a habit of getting yourself into trouble, don't you? First that business in the summer, then that slimy councillor at the museum, and now this.' Dora made her way out of the cubicle. 'It isn't normal.' She called back through the curtain, 'You need to get a grip.'

Liz almost laughed.

LIZ MANAGED to convince the doctor that, as a former nurse, she knew all the signs of post-concussion complications and would keep an eye on herself. They put a couple of staples in her forehead, and by lunchtime, she was on her way home in a taxi.

She had a lot to think about. Had someone tried to kill her? The shove in her back had been too violent to be accidental. There had been quite a few people waiting to cross – one of them had definitely tried to hurt her. But who? The scarred man? Or someone else? She thought she'd been discreet in her blackmail investigation, but perhaps she'd simply got too close to the killer for comfort. There were a lot more questions than answers, but one thing was very clear – she had to tell Kevin what was going on. But first she needed to give Gillian and Grazyna fair warning. Once the list was in police hands, they would become suspects.

Poor Nelson had had an accident in the cottage – she'd been away too long. He didn't bark or even get out of his basket when he heard her key in the door, just ignored her completely. He clearly blamed her for what had happened. Which was fair enough. She mopped up the puddle and took him for a short walk down to the shore. Then, when she'd settled him down again, she prepared herself for the climb up to St Mary's.

By the time she'd reached the top of the abbey steps, she was feeling dizzy and a little sick. She sat for a while by St Caedmon's cross to get her breath back, then set off again along the clifftop to the church.

She found Gillian sweeping out the entrance porch.

'I wouldn't let Iris come to work,' she said to Liz, by way of explanation. 'She says there's nothing wrong with her, but I wouldn't be able to live with myself if she had another turn coming up the steps.' She took a closer look at Liz. 'What on earth have you done to your head?'

'It's nothing. Just a bump.'

'You're as bad as Iris. Should you even be out?'

'I wanted a word.'

Gillian took in Liz's solemn expression. 'Sounds ominous.'

Liz could hear voices in the church. Sightseers, probably. She didn't want to be overheard.

'It needs to be private. Is there somewhere we can go?'

Gillian nodded, propped her broom against the wall, and led Liz into the church, across the nave, and into the vestry. It was a tiny room, with some of Gillian's ecclesiastical vestments hanging on a rail in a corner, and a couple of tatty armchairs. There was also a kettle on a tray with a carton of milk.

'Would you like a cuppa?' asked Gillian. 'The milk's fresh.'

Liz shook her head.

Gillian frowned. 'Oh dear. It must be serious.'

Liz didn't deny it. They settled themselves in the chairs. Gillian looked at her expectantly. Liz took a deep breath. There was no easy way to say this.

'I know you're being blackmailed.'

Gillian recoiled as if Liz had slapped her. If Liz had had any doubts before that the list was of blackmail victims, she had none now.

She plunged on. 'It was Satterthwaite. I found his list of victims. And a letter he sent to... someone else.'

Gillian blinked. Her face had drained of colour.

Liz rushed to reassure her. 'I have no idea what he was blackmailing you about.'

Gillian covered her face with her hands. She was silent for a long minute.

Finally she spoke. 'It's over. Thank God.'

Liz squirmed. 'I'm afraid not.'

Gillian lowered her hands and stared at her. Her cheeks were wet.

'The thing is,' continued Liz, 'I have to give the list to the police. They need to know what's going on. I really should have given it to them straightaway. But I wanted to let you know... to warn you. They're bound to ask questions.'

Gillian exhaled a long, shaky breath. '"Be sure your sin will find you out."'

A quote from the Bible. 'I'm sorry.'

Gillian stood up suddenly. She went to a cupboard in the corner and took out two glasses and a bottle of malt whisky. She put a generous splash into each glass and handed one to Liz.

'Lagavulin,' she said. 'Special occasions only.'

Liz really didn't want it. She shouldn't drink alcohol after a concussion, but didn't want to be rude and refuse. Gillian sat down again and took a deep breath.

'When I was twenty-one –' she began.

Liz interrupted. 'You don't have to tell me.'

Gillian gave a shaky laugh. 'The strange thing is I *want* to tell you. It'll be a relief after all these years. And I might as well practice, for the police.' She met Liz's eye. 'I had a baby. Fresh out of theological college. It was an accident... obviously.' She sighed. 'I gave it away.'

That took a few moments to sink in. 'You never told anyone?'

'Only my mum. She was horrified. Convinced me I was doing the right thing.'

'How awful.'

'I haven't regretted it. Not really. I wouldn't have been a

good mother, not back then. Maybe not even now. And I was just starting out. It would have derailed my career in the church before it had properly begun.' Gillian took a large gulp of whisky that caught her throat and made her gasp. Her voice was hoarse when she spoke again. 'But I'm not proud of it. I know some members of my congregation would condemn me, maybe even lobby the bishop to have me removed. It wasn't a risk I was prepared to take.'

'So you paid him?'

Gillian nodded. 'I had no idea it was Satterthwaite. And now he's dead. It's a relief... God help me, is that a terrible thing to say?'

'No. Of course not. You're only human.'

Gillian nodded sadly. 'Benedict will find out now, won't he?'

Liz wasn't sure how to respond to that.

'If I tell the police what happened,' continued Gillian, 'Kevin will know. And he'll tell his dad.'

'Not necessarily. I'm sure he wouldn't say anything if you asked him not to.'

Gillian shook her head. 'Nothing stays a secret in this town for long.'

'So why not tell Benedict yourself? A pre-emptive strike?'

'I can't do that.' Gillian met Liz's eye. 'I just can't.'

'Then you're a bit screwed, aren't you?' said Liz gently.

Gillian gave a wry laugh. 'Just a bit. Do you really have to take the list to the police?'

Liz pulled a sorry face. 'Satterthwaite's murder is probably connected to his blackmail. And since I found the list, things have... escalated.' She didn't want to tell Gillian she thought someone was trying to kill her. Gillian had more than enough on her own plate.

Gillian nodded. 'Thanks for giving me a heads-up, Liz. It can't have been easy.'

Liz didn't deny it. She thought it was a real mark of class that Gillian could worry about someone else in the middle of all her own troubles.

GRAZYNA WAS next on Liz's list. Liz knew she was due a break at the Full Moon at three thirty, when she usually went outside to have an e-cigarette. She hurried back down the abbey steps, along Church Street and into Sandgate, where she lingered in the alley behind the café for Grazyna to come out. She didn't have to wait long before a tall figure emerged from the kitchen doorway.

'Liz!' she exclaimed when she saw her. 'What happened to your head?'

'Just a bump.' It was aching, though, and she still felt nauseous.

'What are you doing loitering out here?' Loitering. Grazyna's English really was good.

'Waiting for a word with you, actually.'

'Oh?' Grazyna's expression grew wary. 'What about?'

'A couple of things. Fancy a walk?'

They went down the alley to the foreshore, the scene of Liz and Nelson's frantic dash to escape the scarred man. A lone seagull wailed somewhere above them, and pebbles crunched under their feet as they walked.

'I saw Mike Howson this morning,' said Liz.

'Who?'

'Mike the fishmonger. He seems to think Lukasz and Eryk might be playing truant.'

Grazyna grimaced and sighed. 'Those boys.' She took out her e-cigarette, looked at it, then pushed it back into her pocket. 'They will be the death of me.'

'Talking of death –' it was a bumpy segue into the main reason for Liz's visit, but would have to do '– do you remember Donnie Satterthwaite, the man who was murdered?

'Of course.'

'It turns out he was blackmailing people.' Liz glanced at Grazyna's face. She could only see it in profile, but there wasn't a flicker of emotion there, not even surprise.

'There's a list,' continued Liz, 'of people he was black-mailing.'

Still nothing.

Liz decided to go for it. 'You're on the list, Grazyna.'

Grazyna raised her dark brows. 'Strange.'

'Strange?'

'I am not being blackmailed, Liz.'

'You're sure?'

'I think I would know, don't you?' She stopped and turned to face her. 'I have no secrets. No secrets at all.'

Liz didn't believe her. Only someone with something to hide would keep their expression so eerily blank. It was as if a steel shutter had come down.

'Well, that's a relief,' lied Liz. 'I thought I should let you know, just in case.'

'You have discovered all this how?' asked Grazyna.

Liz didn't want to mention the part the boys had played – she'd already grassed them up once – so decided brevity was the best strategy. 'Because I have... I had... the list. The police have it now.'

'I see.' Grazyna nodded, then shrugged. 'It is a mystery.'

'I daresay the police will want to talk to you.'

'They are very welcome to. As I said, I have no secrets.' Grazyna gave a smile that failed to reach her eyes. 'And now I must get back to the café.'

Liz watched her stride back the way they had come – a tall, solitary figure against the grey shore. She wasn't sure why she'd lied to Grazyna about not having the list anymore.

Was it because she felt guilty she still had it? Or because Grazyna's poker face had disturbed her more than she cared to admit? Either way it was interesting and a little worrying that her own instincts for self-preservation had cut in.

She hurried back to Gull Cottage, where Nelson greeted her with his usual 'yip'. She was glad he'd forgiven her for his earlier slip. She gave him his tea, then clipped him onto his lead for a walk.

Halfway up the abbey steps, Liz paused to catch her breath on one of the coffin steps as usual, but she didn't admire the view as she normally did. Her head was pounding. She'd meant to take some painkillers before she came out, but had forgotten. Trying to ignore the pain, she took out her mobile phone and dialled. It rang, then went to answerphone.

'Kevin, it's Liz. Can we meet in our usual spot in an hour? I have something I need to tell you.'

14

'**Y**ou can't be serious?'

Their 'usual spot' was one of the all-weather shelters on the West Cliff, where they often met to eat a packed lunch together. The beach lay below, and the vast grey horizon of the North Sea stretched out in front of them, but the only thing Kevin Ossett had eyes for was the papers Liz had given him.

Liz didn't think his comment was really a question, so waited for him to say something else. She waited quite a while.

'When exactly did the boys give you these?'

'Last Sunday.'

Kevin looked up, aghast. 'But that was almost a week ago! Liz, what were you thinking?'

'I wanted to help Gillian and Grazyna.'

'How? How did you think you could help them?'

'I wanted to see if I could...' She tailed off. 'I didn't want...' She sighed. 'I have no idea.'

Kevin put the list and the blackmail letter into an

evidence bag he took from his pocket. He ran a hand through his hair.

'Flint's going to go ballistic. She'll want to talk to you, and we'll have to bring Eryk and Lukasz in again.'

'Really?' Liz was dismayed.

'We have to find out exactly where they found these,' said Kevin.

'I've already told you. They saw Satterthwaite deliver the letter, and found the list in his cottage in Neptune Yard. Is there no way we can keep the boys out of this?' She wasn't concerned for herself.

'I don't see how.'

They both stared out over the sea for a while. Eventually Kevin spoke again.

'All the people on the list had a motive for killing Satterthwaite. I suppose you've been looking into them?'

Liz thought about denying it, and then decided not to bother. Kevin knew her too well.

'I don't know anything about Emma Summers, but Marty Davidson's been having trouble at his restaurant. Someone deliberately infested it with rats. Nethergate is as shady as they come – he really doesn't like people asking questions. And Charlie Johnson's been taking bribes.'

Kevin's eyes widened. 'Bribes?'

'In exchange for drinks licences.'

He grimaced. 'Tilly?'

Liz nodded.

'What about Gillian and Grazyna?'

'I do know why Gillian was being blackmailed, but I'm not going to tell you. If she wants to tell you, she will. Grazyna...' Liz shrugged. 'Who knows? I asked her, and she denied Satterthwaite was blackmailing her at all.'

'Marty Davidson,' mused Kevin. 'Do you think he was the

MD who came to tea on the night Satterthwaite was poisoned?'

'I don't know.' Liz doubted it. 'From what I can see, he's a hardworking guy who's struggling to make his business work.'

'Who do you think might have done it, then?'

'Well, it's always possible none of them killed Satterthwaite. But if I had to put money on it... I would say Nethergate or Johnson.' Her forehead was still throbbing. She put a hand to it.

Kevin peered at her staples.

'That's a nasty cut you have there. How did you say it happened, again?'

'I tripped over the kerb.'

'Hmm.' Kevin narrowed his eyes at her. 'If you say so.'

'WHY IS IT, Mrs McLuckie, that you insist on getting involved in my investigations, even when they have nothing to do with you?' Detective Inspector Flint glared over the interview table at Liz. She and Constable Williams had taken a statement from Liz about how the blackmail list and the letter had come into her possession. 'You do realise that by holding on to this evidence, you may have hampered our murder investigation?'

Liz nodded.

'I should charge you with interfering in a criminal investigation.'

Liz doubted she would, but nodded again, hoping she looked suitably contrite. She obviously didn't, because Flint narrowed her eyes.

'Constable Williams, arrest Mrs McLuckie.'

Williams and Liz stared at Flint in shock.

Flint nodded at Williams. 'Go on.'

'Mrs McLuckie,' he began, 'I'm arresting you for...' He stopped and looked at Flint.

'Interfering in a criminal investigation.'

'... for interfering in a criminal investigation,' Williams continued, with an unhappy expression. 'You do not have to say anything, but...'

'Enough!' Flint gave Liz a cold smile. 'Isn't very nice, is it? Next time, it'll be for real. Williams, see Mrs McLuckie out, and send in the boys and their mother.'

'I BET it isn't even a proper charge,' said Liz. 'Interfering in a criminal investigation.'

Tilly shrugged. 'I really don't know.'

The café was quiet – the lull between teatime and the evening rush. Mags put a mug of tea in front of Liz.

'Why didn't you tell us any of this was going on?' she asked.

'I couldn't really, not without dropping Eryk and Lukasz in it.'

'Well they're in it now, right enough. Up to their necks.' Mags put her hand on Tilly's shoulder, and Tilly gave it a squeeze. They'd obviously patched things up between them. Liz was glad.

'Who did you say was on the list apart from Grazyna and Gillian?' asked Mags.

'Marty Davidson, Emma Summers, Philip Nethergate and Charlie Johnson.'

Tilly shuddered at the last name. 'Doesn't take a genius to work out what *he* was being blackmailed about.'

'But is he a murderer?' asked Mags. 'I can't see it, myself.'

Liz could. Johnson was an ambitious man, and she knew from past experience that almost anyone could commit murder, given the right motivation. You never really knew what was going on in someone else's head.

'What are you going to do now?' asked Tilly.

'Absolutely nothing,' said Liz. 'Flint will be on me like a ton of bricks if I so much as breathe in the direction of her investigation.'

'That's a pity,' said Tilly. 'I do like a good murder.'

Mags shot her a warning look. 'Tilly...'

Tilly held up her hands. 'Don't worry, I'm keeping out of it. I learned my lesson last time.'

'I'm pleased to hear it.' Mags nodded at Liz. 'And it's probably not a bad thing Sherlock here is done with it too.'

Liz realised she meant her. She laughed. 'You're probably right.'

'I *am* right.' Mags headed out through the beaded curtain.

Liz finished her tea. 'Got to get back to Nelson. He peed on the floor earlier. He'll never forgive me if he has to do it again.' She stood up... and then had to sit down again, fast.

'Are you okay?' asked Tilly, face creased with concern.

'Just a bit dizzy. I'll be alright in a minute.'

'I'm surprised the hospital let you out.' She peered at Liz's head. 'That looks nasty.'

'I'm fine. I just need to go home and put my feet up.'

'I'd walk back with you, but there's only me serving.'

'Don't worry, I'll take it slowly. I'll be fine.'

She kept her promise and walked slowly back to Gull Cottage. The narrow streets of the town were relatively empty – all the Goth visitors were in their accommodation, getting ready for Friday night revelry. Liz enjoyed not having to jostle and weave on the narrow pavement for once. She'd overstretched herself since she'd left the hospital – she'd spoken to Gillian, Grazyna and Kevin, and had been grilled by DI Flint. It was hardly surprising she felt a bit fragile.

Nelson was oddly silent when she put the key in the lock

of Gull Cottage. Had he peed again? To her surprise, there was no sign of him in the kitchen, but there was a note on the kitchen table from Niall.

Have taken N for a walk. Back soon.

What a star. Liz never knew when she'd find Niall at home. He was working odd shifts at the Duke of York and also spending a lot of time out and about selling T-shirts and making new friends in his Bride of Frankenstein costume. But it was still a comfort knowing she wasn't completely on her own in the cottage.

She took her coat off and sat at the kitchen table. Every inch of her ached. She really should make herself something to eat – she couldn't actually remember when she'd last eaten anything – but somehow she couldn't summon the energy to do it. Instead, she sat and stared into space.

There was a knock at the door.

Liz sighed and heaved herself out of the chair.

Charlie Johnson beamed at her from the doorstep. He was wearing checked trousers and a golfing shirt that barely stretched over his paunch. His arms were full of roses. Liz's spirits sank even lower.

'Liz! I heard you'd been in the hospital. I was on my way to the club and thought I'd call on the way, to make sure you were alright.' His smile was broad, but his blue eyes drilled into her.

'I'm fine, thank you.'

'Did you get my other roses? And my message?'

'Yes, thank you.'

'So?'

'So?'

'Will you let me take you to dinner? There's a very special restaurant I know in York. We could stay over.'

Liz's instinctive response was to slam the door in his face, but she just didn't have the energy.

'I don't think so.'

Johnson looked disappointed. 'Maybe when you're feeling better?' He gave her the roses. 'I'll leave these with you.'

She didn't say anything more, but took the roses and closed the door, ignoring his expression of dismay. She put the roses on the table. She had no idea what she was going to do with them. There were no more vases left, and their sweet scent was starting to make her feel sick.

There was another knock on the door.

Liz sighed. Couldn't the man take a hint? Did she have to spell it out?

She opened the door... and gasped. She immediately tried to slam it shut again. But a black boot had wedged itself against the door and the frame. It opened inexorably wider, to reveal a stubbled face.

'Not so fast,' said the scarred man. 'We need a word.'

Realising she wasn't going to get the door closed again, she retreated quickly into the kitchen, putting the table between them as he barged inside.

The man spotted the roses. 'Someone's popular,' he said. He bent to take a sniff. 'Very nice.' He looked around. 'You own this cottage and the one next door, don't you?'

'None of your business. Stop playing games and say what you want to say.'

'Right to the nub of the matter, eh?' He shrugged. 'Suits me. You know who I work for?'

'Philip Nethergate.'

'Exactly. The man you've been asking questions about. Mr Nethergate has worked hard to get where he is, and won't stand for anyone sticking their nose into his business... particularly his *financial* business. Get me?'

Financial? 'Not really, no.'

'He's not going to give his money to any Tom, Dick or Harry who threatens him.'

'Threatens...?' Liz realised, with some alarm, what was going on. '*I'm* not the one who's been blackmailing him.'

The man gave her a sceptical look.

'It was Donnie Satterthwaite.'

'So why have *you* been poking your nose in?'

'Satterthwaite had a list. Of people he was blackmailing. Your boss was on it.'

'A list?' The man rubbed a hand over his stubbled chin. 'Where is it now?'

'The police have it.'

The man scowled. 'Are you on the list too?' he asked.

'No. But friends of mine are.'

He nodded. 'Well, take my advice, Mrs Nosy Parker, and mind your own business. Or you might have another accident.'

Indignation flashed through Liz. 'Was it you who pushed me?'

The man grinned. 'You should be more careful.'

He snapped a rose off the bunch on the table, put it into the buttonhole of his leather jacket, and left.

Liz sat down shakily. The nerve of the man, to push his way in like that! It seemed likely now that he had shoved her into the road, but there was no way of knowing for sure. One thing *was* clear, however – if Nethergate didn't know Satterthwaite was the blackmailer, he would have had no reason to poison him.

THAT NIGHT NIALL had another shift at the Duke, so Liz surrendered to her aches and pains and had an early night. After taking Nelson out for his final pee, she took two painkillers and settled herself into bed with cocoa and the latest procedural crime thriller from her favourite author. It probably wasn't the best genre to take her mind off things, but she liked that the series had a female detective and was set in the North of England. There was a certain comfort in it in spite of the bloody crimes.

After twenty minutes or so, however, Liz realised she hadn't taken in the last two paragraphs and had probably missed something vital. Real-life events were going around and around in her head, eclipsing fiction. She wondered how Grazyna and the boys had got on at the police station, and whether Flint had spoken to any of the other names on the list. Should she tell Kevin he could eliminate Nethergate? If she did, she would also have to tell him about Nethergate's henchman and the possibility he had pushed her into the road. It was a whole can of worms she would prefer not to open if she could help it.

If Philip Nethergate hadn't poisoned Satterthwaite, who had? The list of suspects was shorter now, and Charlie Johnson was right at the top.

Although, Marty Davidson still wasn't in the clear. Was he the mysterious MD who'd come to tea the night Satterthwaite was murdered...?

WHEN SHE WOKE, moonlight was pouring into her bedroom through her roof window. Her novel lay open on the cover, and she still had her reading glasses on. She had drifted off. Disorientated, she looked at her watch. Half past one. She felt as if she hadn't come out of sleep naturally, but had been dragged out of it. Had something woken her?

She took her glasses off and reached to switch off the bedside light. As she did, a howl came from somewhere outside. She stopped, her arm in mid-air, all the hairs on it prickling to attention.

There was a moment's silence; then it came again. A long, mournful sound. It was answered almost immediately by another, this one louder and more guttural that came from downstairs. Nelson.

Something pattered onto the glass of the roof window, making Liz jump. Shale and dirt, from the cliff. Was there something up there? She scrambled out of bed and peered up through the window. She couldn't see anything moving in the inky darkness above. Surely it wasn't the boys? The cliff was too steep and dangerous, and hadn't they promised Flint they would stop their nocturnal howling?

Nelson gave another wail downstairs in the kitchen. She could hear his claws scrabbling at the front door. She threw on her dressing gown and hurried down the rickety stairs. By the time she reached the kitchen, Nelson was hurling himself against the door. She was scared he would hurt himself.

'It's okay. It's okay.' She made a grab for him and held him against her. 'It's okay.'

The whole of his body was trembling, although whether it was with fight or flight she had no way of knowing. She held him until she felt his tremors subside.

'Can I let you go now? Are you okay?'

She decided to risk it. He continued to listen at the door, ears pricked, but didn't throw himself against it again. He gave her a sideways, slightly apologetic look.

Although she knew Nelson liked to sleep on her bed, she rarely allowed it. She firmly believed they should have their own space. Tonight, however, she decided to make an exception, but whether it was for his sake or for hers she wasn't quite sure. She snuggled Nelson's furry body close under the duvet until she eventually slipped into sleep.

15

'I saw it! I saw it, Mrs McLuckie. I saw the Barghest!' Neville took the breakfast basket from her and ushered her into Gull Cottage. Jackie was sitting in her pyjamas, round-eyed with excitement.

'Did you hear it last night?' she asked.

Liz nodded. 'About half past one? Nelson wasn't happy.'

'It gave me goose bumps all over,' said Jackie. 'I didn't dare look out the window.'

'I did!' said Neville. 'After we heard the howling, I came downstairs to get a drink, and I heard something outside. I looked out the kitchen window... right here... and I saw it. It was huge! Big, black and shaggy, just walking down the middle of the street!'

'I thought he was going to have a heart attack, he was that excited.'

Liz eyed Neville. He still looked a bit overstimulated – red-faced and full of nervous energy.

'We're going to go to the *Bugle* this morning,' said Jackie, 'to tell them all about it. Do you know where the office is?'

'Flowergate, I think. Above the Building Society.'

'We'll wear our normal clothes. So they take us seriously.'

That was definitely a good idea. Tales of demon dogs were incredible enough without coming from Sweeney Todd and Mrs Lovett. Quite a few other people would also have heard the howls, however. The *Bugle*'s phones were likely to be ringing off the hook.

'We'll have our breakfast first,' said Jackie. 'And then we'll go.' She started to unpack the basket. 'Oh, blackberry jam this morning. My favourite.'

But Neville wasn't ready to stop talking about the Barghest. 'I still can't believe I saw it. This is the best holiday ever!'

'It's not completely good news, though, is it?' said Jackie solemnly. 'For someone. I mean... who's going to die this time?'

Liz retreated to Gull Cottage. She was making her own breakfast – toast and marmalade – when there was a knock at the door.

Yip, yip, yip. Nelson jumped out of his basket and ran to the door.

Liz hesitated. She had Nelson, and Niall was asleep in bed upstairs – well within shouting distance – but her heart was still thumping as she opened the door. To her surprise, it was Peggy Satterthwaite and Emma Summers. Peggy was holding a bouquet of colourful freesias.

'Dora told us about your accident, so we thought we would come and see how you were,' said Emma.

'You were so kind to return my glove the other day,' added Peggy.

Liz recovered from her surprise. 'Come in, please.'

'These are for you,' Peggy said, handing over the freesias. 'Oh!' she said as she came into the kitchen. 'I see someone else had the same idea.' She was looking at Charlie Johnson's roses, some of which were a little wilted. Liz made a mental note to ditch them.

'You have an admirer,' said Emma. 'How lovely.'

Liz said nothing and sniffed the freesias. They had a delicious, wine-like scent.

'I grow them in my greenhouse,' said Emma. 'They're not usually in bloom this time of year.'

'They're lovely. Thank you. Would you both like tea?'

Peggy shook her head. 'We're just on our way to the *Bugle*. They've asked me to pop in before the football match tomorrow.' She looked wistful. 'My Donnie was their star player, you know.'

Liz had forgotten about the football match. On the last day of the festival it was traditional for a team of locals, put together by the *Bugle*, to play a game against a team of visiting Goths. This year Niall was going to play for the Goth team because, strictly speaking, he was a visitor.

'Donnie had a marvellous left foot,' said Peggy. 'He was terribly dyslexic, but a very good football player.'

'You must have been so proud,' said Liz, 'that he overcame his challenges to become a journalist.'

'Oh, once Donnie set his mind to something, there was no stopping him.' Peggy paused and stared off into space. Emma looked ruefully at Liz.

Liz wondered whether she'd done the right thing, engaging Peggy in conversation about her dead son. It was always hard to know what to say to the recently bereaved. When Mark had died, many people – even some of their oldest friends – had avoided talking about him at all. That had put huge swathes of their shared experiences out of bounds, and resulted in some very awkward interactions. Unfortunately, some of their friends had just found it all too awkward to deal with, and had melted away. Liz still missed them sometimes.

'But how's your poor head?' Emma asked, pulling everyone back to the present day.

'Not too bad. It was just a bump.'

'Dora said it could have been much worse.'

'It could,' agreed Liz. 'She probably saved my life.' She should give credit where it was due.

Peggy peered at Liz's stapled forehead and tutted. 'That looks sore. I have some arnica cream at home. It's marvellous for bruises. I'll bring some round for you.'

'You don't need to do that,' protested Liz. 'I can buy some at the chemist.'

'Don't be silly, it's no trouble at all.' Peggy smiled, then looked at her watch. 'Oh... we must dash.'

'Are you both going to the match tomorrow?'

'I shouldn't think so,' said Emma. She looked at Peggy for confirmation.

'No. I wouldn't want to spoil things. No one likes a spectre at the feast, do they?'

Liz decided she liked Peggy. Not many people would put themselves to so much trouble for a stranger, especially when they'd just lost their son in such a terrible way. She liked Emma too. It was lucky that Peggy had such a good friend to support her.

In the Full Moon café, the customers were buzzing about the Barghest, like bees in a hive. Iris was sitting in her usual seat, holding court to a table of sooty believers.

'I TOLD YOU, DIDN'T I?' she bellowed as Liz passed. 'I TOLD YOU IT WAS THE BARGHEST. AND NOW IT'S COME AGAIN. WHO HAS IT COME FOR THIS TIME?'

Liz saw that Irwin was also sitting at the table, with a cappuccino and a long-suffering expression. She gave him a wave. He raised an ironic eyebrow in her direction.

'Is Grazyna in this morning?' she asked Tilly, who was serving at the counter, in her scarlet cape.

'In the kitchen.' Tilly grinned. 'The boys have really stirred things up again, haven't they? I'm not complaining, though. We've never been so busy.'

Liz went through to the kitchen, where Mags was making soup, and Grazyna was cutting a delicious-looking traybake into slices. As soon as Grazyna saw Liz, she threw up her hands.

'It wasn't them,' she said. 'They were in bed.'

'Are you sure?'

'I sent them up early, as a punishment, after we got in from the police station. I checked them at half past midnight. They were both asleep.'

Liz wondered how Grazyna had got on with Flint and Kevin. Had they questioned her about the blackmail list? But it wasn't really the time to ask, and was none of her business anyway.

'So who was howling?' she asked instead.

'Maybe it isn't *who*,' said Mags. 'Maybe it really is a *what*. Perhaps the Barghest is real?'

'There is no such thing,' said Grazyna. 'And besides, it is too much of a coincidence that this demon suddenly decides to appear when my boys are imitating it.'

'Perhaps they summoned it somehow?' said Mags mischievously. 'Summoning demons by accident happens all the time in horror movies.'

'I think not,' said Grazyna.

Mags continued to stir her soup. 'Iris did see it, though, didn't she?'

Grazyna sniffed.

'Neville saw it too,' said Liz. 'Last night.'

Mags stopped stirring. 'What?'

'Who is Neville?' demanded Grazyna.

'One of my Kipper Cottage guests. He said he looked out of the window and saw it in Henrietta Street.'

'There you go, then,' said Mags, in triumph.

'Surely you do not believe him?'

'I do, actually,' admitted Liz. 'I believe Iris too. They're both convinced they saw something.'

'A cat,' said Grazyna. 'Or a dog. An ordinary dog.'

Liz doubted it. Iris's and Neville's descriptions didn't sound like someone's pet, but Grazyna's tone was too decisive to argue with.

16

'What are you doing that there for?' When Liz got back to Gull Cottage, Niall was cleaning his football boots on the kitchen table.

'Where do you want me to do it?'

'I don't know. On the floor somewhere?'

'I'm nearly done now. And I put newspaper down.'

Liz saw all the dirt from the boots was confined to a sheet of newspaper, so she gave up the argument. 'Would you like half my toastie?'

'Only if you're sure. I don't want to rob you.'

'I'd have got one for you if I'd known you were up.' A thought occurred to her. 'How did you sleep last night?'

'Grand.'

'You didn't hear anything?'

Niall looked up from his boots. 'Should I have?'

'The Barghest was back. I heard it. Nelson did too. I'm surprised you didn't hear him, he made such a racket.'

Niall looked disappointed. 'I didn't hear a thing. I must admit I'd had a couple of pints, though. Didn't so much fall asleep as pass out.'

Liz wasn't sure how she felt about that. Having Niall in the house had made her feel safer. She wouldn't have felt quite so secure if she'd known he was practically unconscious. She divided her toastie in half and put it onto two plates, then put the kettle on for Niall. While she waited for it to boil, she started putting the roses into a bin bag.

'That's a shame,' said Niall. 'They're still ok.'

'I'm just fed up with them.'

Niall raised his eyebrows. 'Fallen out with him, have you? Whoever he is?'

'I was never "in" with him in the first place.' She decided a change of subject was in order. 'The kettle's boiled, if you want to make yourself a cup of tea.'

Niall cleared the table so she could sit to eat her toastie and drink her coffee. He made himself a mug of tea and joined her. It was the first time all week he'd actually stayed still for more than two minutes. She saw he was pale and had shadows under his eyes.

'Are you okay?' she asked.

'Me? I'm grand. Just burning the candle at both ends is all.'

'Perhaps you shouldn't be doing so many shifts at the Duke? You're supposed to be on holiday.'

Niall shrugged. 'I need the cash.'

'Your new job starts the week after next, doesn't it?' Niall had found himself a fixed-term contract at the Museum of Liverpool until Christmas. 'You must be looking forward to it.'

'Suppose.'

Liz was taken aback by his lacklustre response. The last time he'd mentioned it, he'd been full of enthusiasm. She frowned.

'You *are* still going to Liverpool?'

'As far as I know.' A strangely cryptic response. He pushed

his chair back. 'Thanks for the toastie. Got to dash. I have a training session.'

'Good luck.'

When he'd gone, Liz finished her coffee. Was Niall's Liverpool contract in doubt? If so, why wouldn't he tell her about it? He wasn't usually so guarded. She supposed he would tell her when he was ready, and in the meantime, she'd just have to make herself available for him to talk if he wanted to.

What was she going to do with the rest of the day? She still felt fragile after her fall, so whatever it was, it couldn't be too energetic. She supposed she should be starting to think about the renovations at Gull Cottage now that Kipper was finished, but even just looking around the kitchen, with its worn-out units, cheap wall panelling and swirly-patterned carpet, was bringing on another headache. She decided to take herself up to the sitting room to do some research.

'Are you coming, Nelson?'

He jumped out of his basket, and she carried it up to the sitting room on the first floor. She should get a second basket to keep up there permanently, which would save her lugging this one up and down.

Liz switched on her laptop. She needed new light fittings for the kitchen and quite fancied bulkhead-style wall lights, the kind you got on boats. But she couldn't resist looking at dog baskets first. She found a nice one made from woven rattan, but it was quite pricey, so she bookmarked it for her attention at some time in the hopefully not-too-distant future. Then she started her search for lights.

She was soon discouraged.

Original reclaimed bulkhead lights were scarily expensive, and all the reproduction ones looked flimsy in comparison. She sighed and stared out of her window. Why was everything so expensive?

The screen was making her head ache, so she switched her laptop off and looked around for something else to do. She spotted the bookshop bag on the sofa and took out her copy of Emma Summer's autobiography, *Blood Sister*. The photo on the front showed Emma in her heyday, dark eyed and sinister as Alyssa the Vampyre. Liz found her reading glasses and settled herself down to read.

I come from a long line of seafaring folk, stretching all the way back to the eighteenth century. My father always said we should have been born with flippers and gills, a joke that never found favour with my mother, an accountant's daughter, who thought herself above such vulgar jests. I was named after my paternal grandmother, Michele. She met her husband, George Donoghue, in the fishing village of Seahouses, on the Northumberland coast...

Liz sat up. She read the lines again, just to be sure. Michele was Emma's *paternal* grandmother, so... Emma Summers must be a stage name. Her real name was Michele Donoghue. MD.

Liz snapped the book shut and took off her glasses. Surely not? Was Emma the person Satterthwaite had invited to tea? If so, why had he been so cryptic on his calendar?

It was a long shot – Liz couldn't think of anyone less like a murderer than Emma – but it was too much of a coincidence to be ignored.

She tried to remember where Emma said she lived.

'Towards Ruswarp.'

Not 'in' Ruswarp, but 'towards' it. There was only one road that headed out of town in that direction. Liz switched her laptop on again and went online to look at a satellite image of Ruswarp Lane.

It was mostly small to medium-sized houses on the lane,

apart from one big Victorian building set back from the main road and accessed by a driveway. It had an old-fashioned glasshouse running the length of one of the garden walls. Emma had said she'd grown the freesias in her greenhouse.

Forgetting all her good intentions not to exert herself, Liz went downstairs to get her coat. At the last minute, she decided to take Nelson with her. It would do them both good.

Thirty-five minutes after leaving Gull Cottage, she and Nelson turned off Mayfield Road into Ruswarp Lane, a minor road that ran all the way down to Ruswarp village, about a mile or so away. She knew from the satellite image that the big house was about a quarter of a mile down it, on the left-hand side. She found it easily. The sign said Staithes House, and the gates were open.

Liz hesitated. She probably should have called Kevin to tell him what she'd discovered. On the other hand, she didn't really believe that Emma was the poisoner – it was probably just a coincidence that her real name started with the initials MD. It wasn't Liz's intention to unmask Emma as a killer, just to eliminate her as a suspect. How she was going to manage that, she had no idea.

'Ready, Nelson?'

Nelson cocked an ear.

'Let's go.'

They set off down the gravel drive. It was very neatly kept, flanked by big shrubs Liz thought were rhododendrons. After about seventy yards or so, the drive broadened out into a parking area, where a silver Subaru was parked. The house itself was a large Victorian, with bay windows and a turret. It might have looked rather forbidding if it hadn't been for the abundance of pale-pink roses and ivy climbing the walls – further proof that Emma had green thumbs.

Liz stepped up to the imposing front door and rang the bell.

'Here we go,' she said to Nelson under her breath. 'Behave yourself.'

They waited, but no one came. Liz rang the bell again. It was a very big house – perhaps Emma hadn't heard the bell? After another few minutes, Liz realised that no one was going to answer the door. She peered through the stained-glass panel beside it. She couldn't see anyone moving inside, but wasn't going to be discouraged so easily.

'Come on,' she said to Nelson. 'The car's here. She can't be too far away. Maybe she's in the garden?'

They made their way around the back, through a wrought-iron gate. Liz couldn't resist peeping into the first window they came to. It was a study, with overflowing book-cases and a desk. It made Liz think that Emma might have written her autobiography herself rather than using a ghost writer.

At the back of the house was a large patio, with French windows onto it. All the patio furniture had covers on, and many of the pots were looking a little weather-beaten and sad. Liz imagined it would be lovely in the spring and summer. There was still no sign of Emma. Liz spotted an archway in a hedge that looked as if it might lead into the rest of the garden. She steered Nelson in that direction.

'No peeing, mind,' she said to him. 'And definitely no digging.'

On the other side of the archway, the sprawling garden was jaw-droppingly gorgeous, with specimen trees and lushly planted borders unaffected by the late season. There were lots of intriguing paths leading to secret spots – if Emma was doing some gardening, there was every possibility Liz wouldn't be able to see her.

'Hello?' she called out. 'Hello, Emma?'

No answer.

Perhaps she wasn't home after all? Perhaps Emma had

decided to walk into Whitby rather than taking the car? But then Liz saw the glasshouse she'd seen on the satellite image – a traditional Victorian structure that ran the length of one of the boundary walls. The doors were wide open. Liz wasn't a gardener, but even she knew that hothouse doors shouldn't be left open like that.

As she got closer, she saw there was a pair of gardening gloves, secateurs and a trug full of flowers on the gravel. They looked a little wilted.

Why had Emma left them like that, with the doors wide open?

She tried to look through one of the panes of the hothouse, but couldn't see anything through the condensation.

'Hello, Emma? It's Liz McLuckie,' she called in through the doors. No answer. Surely if Emma had been inside, she would have heard her? Liz was starting to feel a bit twitchy. She fastened Nelson's lead to the door handle and went inside.

The heat hit her a few steps in. It was a proper tropical hothouse, with jungle-like planting and condensation running down the panes. She could hear water trickling somewhere, and a beautiful scent teased her nostrils from one of the luscious blooms nearby. Liz ventured farther in, along a small gravelled path. Ordinarily, she would be enjoying the sensory overload, but her twitchy feeling was getting worse. Much worse.

The little pathway led to a clearing in the middle of the glass house, where there was a bench and a fountain. There was still no sign of anyone. There was a pink cardigan lying on the bench and something scattered on the ground – a dozen or so small, round, brown objects. Liz picked one up to inspect it. It looked like a hard, dried date. As she straightened up, something else caught her eye a few feet away, almost hidden by the massive leaves of a plant. At first she thought it was another pile of discarded clothing, but then she realised what it actually was – someone crumpled on the ground.

'Emma!' Liz ran to help her, but only took a step or two before she stopped.

Emma Summers was beyond help.

17

'Detective Inspector Flint's on her way,' said Constable Williams. 'It shouldn't be too long until she gets here.'

Liz sipped the coffee he had conjured from a flask somewhere, grateful for the reprieve, however temporary. She was sitting in the front seat of one of two squad cars now parked in the gravel driveway beside Emma's Subaru, her legs out the door. There was also a van that Liz assumed belonged to the forensics team. They were in the process of unpacking what looked like a garden gazebo, but was more probably the kind of tent she'd seen on the TV news.

She was quite surprised. She'd always assumed such tents were used to keep prying eyes away from the crime scene, but they were on private property, and there wasn't likely to be a crowd. She observed it all with a feeling of detachment, almost as if she *were* watching it on TV. She realised she might be in shock.

Nelson was gazing up at her, forehead wrinkled.

'Don't look so worried,' she said to him.

'Perhaps he's hungry. Would he like a biscuit?' asked

Williams. He produced a digestive biscuit from his pocket. Liz nodded. Nelson accepted the constable's gift daintily.

'I suppose I should probably take a statement,' said Williams.

Liz nodded. 'I suppose so.'

'But only if you're up to it?'

'I'm fine.'

She wasn't completely sure she was, but Williams took her at her word and took his notebook from his pocket.

A black car swung into the driveway and stopped in a spray of gravel. Flint jumped out. She spotted Liz, then Williams, his pen poised over his notebook.

'Not here!' the DI barked. 'Take her to the station, and keep her there until I get back. I'll take her statement myself.' She eyed Nelson with distaste. 'Get animal control to look after the dog.'

Liz had had enough. 'I don't bloody think so!' She jumped out of the car. 'I'm not a suspect. I'm just helping you with your enquiries. Nelson stays with me!'

Flint shrugged. 'Whatever. I'll be there as soon as I can.' She disappeared around the side of the house.

Williams called after the DI. 'Ma'am? DI Flint?'

Her scowling face reappeared. 'What?'

'You'll have to move your car. I can't get the squad car out.'

LIZ CALLED Niall from the car and arranged for him to meet her at the station so he could take Nelson home, which was just as well, because she waited for more than two hours for DI Flint to return. Eventually Flint appeared and took her through to an interview room, where Kevin was already waiting. Kevin met Liz's eye and gave her a rueful look. He looked tired.

They all sat down. Flint took off her jacket. There were

sweat marks under her arms, and her face was tight with tension.

'Let's begin at the beginning,' Flint said. 'Why had you gone to see Emma Summers?'

Liz had been thinking about things a lot while she was waiting, and had decided it was best to come completely clean. 'Because her real name is Michele Donoghue.'

There was a beat of silence.

Liz continued, 'MD. The same as the initials on Satterthwaite's calendar?'

Flint glared at Kevin.

'I didn't tell her!' said Kevin.

'He didn't,' confirmed Liz. 'I saw the calendar myself.'

Flint glared at Liz. 'How?'

'There was a bird. In Satterthwaite's cottage. I helped Constable Williams get it out.'

'Williams let you in the cottage?'

'Yes.' Liz realised, a little late, that she had completely dumped Williams in it. 'He doesn't like birds. It had got in and was making an awful mess of the crime scene.'

Flint stared at her. She pushed her chair back and stood up. She paced the room, trying to find words. 'The people in this town are unbelievable. You all think you're in some kind of bloody murder-solving club.' She jabbed a finger at Liz. 'That's what *policemen* are for!'

'Or *policewomen*,' said Kevin, trying to be helpful.

Flint glared at him. She ran a hand through her hair and sat down again.

'Start again,' she said to Liz. 'Leave nothing out. If I find out later that there's something you've not told me, I'll bloody have you. Got that?'

Liz nodded. 'Got it.'

. . .

AFTERWARDS, Kevin gave Liz a lift home.

'I'm sorry,' she said.

'Don't be daft. It's hardly your fault you found Emma like that. It must have been a shock.'

Liz nodded. That was something of an understatement. 'There was a lot of blood.'

'She took several blows to the back of the head.'

'Any sign of a murder weapon?'

'Not yet. But that's not something you need to worry about.' Kevin took his eyes off the road for a moment to look at her. 'How are you?'

'A bit wobbly. And tired.'

'You should go to bed when you get in. No more adventures today.'

Liz nodded, but then thought of something. 'Someone will have to tell Peggy.'

'Peggy?'

'Peggy Satterthwaite. She and Emma were friends.'

'I'll do it,' said Kevin. 'Give me her address, and I'll call in after I drop you off.'

Liz nodded gratefully. Poor Peggy. First her son, and now her friend. She imagined Peggy would tell Dora. Liz stared out of the window, and her mind went blank for a few minutes. She really was tired.

'I suppose you'll be working late tonight?' she said to Kevin eventually, trying to make conversation.

'I suppose so. And no chance of playing in the match tomorrow.'

He usually played for the local side. They'd be struggling for players, now they'd lost him and Donnie Satterthwaite.

Niall was waiting for her when she got in.

'Nelson's been like a cat on hot bricks. He hasn't settled at all.'

Liz rubbed Nelson's head. 'It's okay. I'm fine. I'm here.' She turned to Niall. 'Sorry I had to dump him on you like that. Were you supposed to be working tonight?'

Niall shrugged. 'Ah, sure, it's no biggie. I could do with an early night myself.'

He still had shadows under his eyes, and his whole demeanour was lacklustre.

'You get yourself to bed, Mrs Mac,' he said, 'and I'll take Nelson out for his last walk.'

'If you're sure.' She hesitated. 'Niall...'

'Mmm?'

'You would tell me, wouldn't you, if there was anything wrong?'

He was taken aback. 'Wrong? Wrong how?'

She shrugged. 'I don't know. Just if there was anything the matter.'

'I'm fine. Honestly. Get yourself up to bed.'

She nodded and made her way wearily up the stairs.

'I'll bring you a cocoa in a minute or two.'

Liz got ready for bed, her mind in a jumble. She was so tired she could barely string two thoughts together. If the murderer was one of Satterthwaite's blackmail victims, why would they kill Emma, another victim? The more she tried to think about it, the less sense it made.

18

The next day dawned dry and clear, perfect for the football match. It was Saturday, the penultimate day of the festival, and the whole town was energised, getting ready for the last burst of celebrations. The match wasn't due to kick off until 2 pm, so Liz spent the morning quietly, trying not to think about Emma Summers. At twelve, she made lunch for herself and Niall and helped him with his Bride of Frankenstein make-up.

'Are you sure you don't want me to take that hem up another inch? You don't want to be tripping over it while you're running.'

'It'll be fine once I've got my boots on. Nothing's going to stop me, Mrs Mac. Did you know my cousin Fergus played for the Ballymun Kickhams?'

'Did he?'

'He was a good player, Fergus. Had to give it up, though. He fell out with the coach over his coke habit.'

'Coke?'

'About thirty cans a day.'

Liz laughed at his bad joke. Niall was doing his best to

jolly himself up, but she wasn't convinced by his performance. If he didn't want to tell her what was troubling him,
there wasn't much she could do about it.

WHITBY TOWN FC's home ground was already crowded
when Liz got there, and had a proper festive atmosphere. The
pop tunes being played by the local brass band were just
about recognisable, and everyone mingled happily. Goth visitors chatted to locals as they stood in line at the fast-food vans
and the beer tent. Liz spotted Neville and Jackie in their
costumes and gave them a wave. Charlie Johnson was also
there, with several other men, including Philip Nethergate.

Liz had never seen Nethergate in the flesh before, but was
able to identify him from the photos she'd seen online, and by
his expensive suit and tie. He was a good-looking man, who
smiled a lot – he didn't really seem like a criminal mastermind.

Liz chided herself. What did she expect? Did she think
he'd bring his own swivel chair and fluffy cat, like a Bond
villain? She looked around for his henchman. She couldn't
see him, but was willing to bet he wouldn't be too far away.
She slid past the group, hoping that Johnson hadn't seen her.

She spotted Tilly and Mags on the far side of the pitch,
beside the hot-dog stall.

'Liz!' Tilly greeted her with a wave. 'Over here!'

'We weren't sure you'd come, after yesterday,' said Mags
when she joined them.

'You've heard about that?'

'Kevin was in the café first thing. What happened?'

'I'll tell you about it later,' Liz said. She really didn't have
the heart – or the stomach – to go into it right then. 'Is
Grazyna holding the fort at the café?'

Mags nodded. 'We've brought Eryk and Lukasz with us, to

get them out of her hair.' She looked around. 'They're here around somewhere.'

'Causing havoc,' said Tilly, wiping mustard off her chin.

As if conjured by their words, the boys suddenly appeared, elbowing their way through the crowd.

'Tilly!' Lukasz tugged on Tilly's sleeve. 'Can we have another hot dog?'

'You've already had two each.'

'Please?' pleaded Eryk.

'Please?'

'Let me buy you one,' said Liz. 'My treat.'

Lukasz's grin frosted into a glare. He sniffed. 'Nah. I don't think I want one now.' He nudged his brother. 'Neither do you, Eryk, do you?'

'Don't I?' Eryk looked astonished, then saw Lukasz's pointed glance at Liz. 'Oh. No. I suppose not.' He looked less than convinced, but Lukasz grabbed his arm and towed him off into the crowd again.

'What was that about?' asked Mags.

'I'm still public enemy number one because I told Kevin about them pretending to be the Barghest,' said Liz. 'I daresay they'll come round eventually.'

'I wouldn't bet on it,' said Tilly. 'Grazyna's talking about leaving.'

'Leaving?' echoed Liz.

Tilly nodded. 'She thinks everyone has it in for the boys. First there was the Barghest thing, and now they're getting blamed for the vandalism in the town. She wants to make a fresh start.'

'That's awful,' said Liz. She could see why the boys were so upset with her.

'It is,' said Tilly gloomily.

'Talking about the Barghest,' said Mags, changing the

subject. 'The prophecy came true, didn't it? There *has* been another death in the town.'

Liz supposed that was true, but doubted the supposedly ghostly dog had anything to do with Emma Summers' death.

Gillian emerged from the crowd beside them, wearing jeans and her clerical collar. 'Emma was supposed to be giving the cup to the winners, but... well, I've had to step in. Does anyone know what happened?'

Tilly and Mags looked at Liz.

Liz was about to confess that she'd been the one who'd found Emma, when she caught sight of Benedict striding towards them.

Gillian saw him too. 'Got to go,' she said hastily. 'Got to mingle.' She made her escape before Benedict could reach them. Tilly met Liz's puzzled look with one of her own.

Benedict joined them. He gave a bleak smile.

'You've just missed Gillian,' said Tilly, fishing.

Benedict looked even bleaker.

Before Tilly and Liz had time to speculate, the brass band struck up an approximation of the *Rocky* theme tune. The teams were coming out!

Everyone crowded to the edge of the pitch. The home team trotted out first, dressed in Whitby Town colours of blue and red. Liz saw a few faces she recognised, including Mike Howson's two sons and Philip Nethergate's scarred henchman. He looked a lot less menacing in shorts.

'We'll be struggling this year,' said a voice beside her. It was Mike, the fishmonger. 'Without Donnie.'

'Was he such a good player?' asked Liz.

'Never seen a left foot like his,' said Mike, 'outside the Premier League.'

Liz wondered. Satterthwaite was dyslexic. Was he also left-handed? She knew that a lot of dyslexic people were; something to do with left brain/right brain function. The thought, which had come to her idly, then crystallised into another, more significant one. She had no time to think it through, however, because the visiting team emerged onto the pitch, to enthusiastic applause from the crowd.

The Goth team was a mix of ordinarily sinister Goths, plus a few more distinctive characters, including an Egyptian mummy, two Draculas and, of course, the Bride of Frankenstein. Niall gave them a thumbs-up as he jogged past. A couple of wolf whistles came from the crowd. Niall curtseyed.

'Drama queen,' said Tilly affectionately.

'Hmm,' said Liz. 'Have you noticed he's been a bit off lately?'

'Off how?' asked Tilly.

Before Liz had time to answer, the referee blew his whistle. The game was on.

The Whitby home team got off to a bad start. Without Satterthwaite in attack and Kevin in defence, they struggled to keep possession of the ball, and went down one nil after just six minutes. The Egyptian mummy and Niall proved a winning combination up front for the visitors, with Niall setting the ball up for the mummy's lethal finishing. When the half-time whistle blew, the visitors were winning three nil. Rather than disappearing into the changing rooms, the teams collapsed onto the pitch, where they were revived with oranges and sausage rolls and rubbed with liniment, where necessary.

Liz remembered the thought that had popped into her head just before kick-off. She scanned the field for the editor of the *Bugle*, who'd given the eulogy at Satterthwaite's memorial, and saw him leaning against one of the goal posts. She made her way over to him.

'Disappointing first half,' she said.

He grunted. 'One way of putting it.'

'You're missing Donnie Satterthwaite.'

He just looked at her.

'I was wondering... isn't it unusual for someone who's dyslexic to become a journalist?'

'Aye, well, there's computers these days, isn't there? Donnie managed well enough.'

'What about writing? Handwriting?'

The editor gave a short laugh. 'Not Donnie. He'd never put pen to paper if he could help it.'

Liz nodded. That was what she suspected. She made her way back to her friends. Why had Satterthwaite *written* the blackmail note to Grazyna? It had been quite fluent, as far as she could remember, with no spelling mistakes or crossing out. The same was true of the list of names.

'Lovely Liz!' Her thoughts were interrupted by a voice she'd been dreading. Charlie Johnson grinned at her over his plastic pint of beer. 'I've been looking for you everywhere.'

'Have you?' she said weakly.

He reached for her arm, but she managed to evade him. 'When are you going to let me take you for that dinner you promised me?'

Promised him?

He lunged for her again, and this time succeeded in grabbing her hand. Dear God, was she going to have to *slap* him?

'Liz!' Benedict appeared out of the crowd. 'Is everything okay?'

'Everything is fine.' Liz wrenched her hand free.

'Johnson.' Benedict nodded coldly at the other man.

'Ossett.' Johnson nodded back, then turned on his heel and strode off in the other direction.

'I hope I didn't interrupt anything?' said Benedict to Liz.

'Interrupt anything?' spluttered Liz. 'Like what?'

Benedict shrugged. 'I don't know. Maybe you and the councillor have a thing going?'

'A thing?' Liz couldn't believe he thought that. Didn't he know her at all?

'I was wondering...' he said, oblivious to his own lack of perception. 'Can I take you for a drink after the match? I need some advice.'

Liz nodded reluctantly. She suspected that advice might have something to do with Gillian.

The home team did better in the second half. They managed to score a goal at sixty minutes, while one of the Draculas was distracted by a trailing bootlace and got a penalty almost at the end, after a foul by the mummy on their goalie. The final score was three-two to the visiting team, a result everyone was more or less happy with. After Gillian had awarded the cup, everyone, including the players, made a beeline for the food vans and the beer tent.

'You ready, Liz?' asked Benedict. 'We can go to the White Horse if you like?'

Liz nodded. 'Hang on a minute. I need the loo first.'

'I'll meet you at the gate.'

Liz made her way to the portable toilets and did the necessary. When she'd finished and washed her hands, she headed for the main gate. Someone stepped into her path, casting a shadow across her. She looked up to see who it was.

'Mrs McLuckie, isn't it?' said Philip Nethergate. He was very tall and even more attractive close up than he had been from a distance. His tan was smooth and golden, his features symmetrical and unnervingly perfect, as if he'd been airbrushed. He held out his perfectly manicured hand for her to shake. 'We've never met.'

'No,' said Liz, ignoring the hand. 'But we do have a mutual acquaintance.'

'Derek, you mean?' Nethergate laughed, showing a very white, very expensive set of teeth. 'Ah, yes. Sorry about Derek. He can be a bit rough around the edges.'

'That's one way of putting it.' Liz was starting to feel nervous. Why had he buttonholed her like that? What did he want? She looked about. There were people everywhere. He couldn't do anything to her there. 'He's told you about Satterthwaite, I suppose? That he was the blackmailer.'

'Keep your voice down!' Nethergate's veneer of affability cracked. 'Yes. He told me, but I'm not sure I believe it.'

Liz gave him a level look. 'Why would I lie about that?'

He shrugged. 'You'd hardly be likely to admit it, would you, if you were the guilty party?'

'I'm not.'

'And you expect me to take your word for it?'

Liz was tired, and her patience was wearing thin. 'I don't expect you to do anything except bugger off and leave me alone. And take that fake smile of yours with you.'

19

The White Horse and Griffin was an ancient coaching inn on Church Street. It was no wider than its doorway at the front, but it went back a long way and broadened out at the rear. They found a table in the narrow, dark-panelled front bar. Benedict seemed distracted, so Liz got the drinks. She bought herself a Jack Daniel's and Coke, and a pint of Marston's Pale Ale for Benedict.

'Your usual,' she said as she put it in front of him. 'If I remember right.'

'Yes. Thanks.' He really didn't seem to be firing on all cylinders.

Liz gulped down her Jack Daniel's. She really needed it after her run-in with Nethergate. Perhaps she shouldn't have goaded him like that? Would he retaliate? It was too late to take it back now.

She saw Benedict was just staring into his glass.

'What was it you wanted to talk to me about?' she asked.

'Gillian's broken up with me.'

She hadn't expected that.

'Last night,' he added.

'I'm sorry.' She was surprised to realise that she actually *was* sorry. She didn't like to see Benedict distressed. 'Did she give you a reason?'

'She said she thought we'd been moving too fast, and that we didn't really have anything in common.' The hurt in his eyes brought a lump to Liz's throat. 'The thing is... that's bull-shit, Liz. We have a lot in common. We were getting on really well. I think there's something else bothering her. Something specific.'

Liz could guess what it was. Gillian was probably trying to distance herself from Benedict in case the news got out about her baby, although Liz didn't understand why she wouldn't just tell him. She couldn't imagine Benedict would judge her harshly – he wasn't that kind of man.

But, of course, she couldn't tell Benedict any of that.

'I don't see how I can help,' she said instead.

'Can you talk to her?'

'Me?'

'She likes you. And she might open up and tell you what's really the problem. I might have done something stupid. Or she might just have the ick.'

'The ick?'

'You know, when you just suddenly go off people for no reason. If that's the case, I'll understand.'

Liz couldn't imagine how anyone would get the ick with Benedict.

'If that's the case,' he said, 'I'll bow out gracefully. But I think there's more to it. If there's anything I can do to put things right, I want to do it.'

'Do you love her?' asked Liz. Her chest tightened.

'It's a bit early for that. When Kate died, I never...' He tailed off, unable to finish the sentence. 'I've only known Gillian a few months, but I'd like to give it a proper chance.'

Liz nodded. 'I'll help if I can. But I doubt she'll say anything to me. It really isn't any of my business, is it?'

'That doesn't usually stop you.'

Liz recoiled.

He realised his mistake. 'I didn't mean that the way it came out. What I meant was, you always like to help if you –'

'That's okay,' she interrupted. 'Honestly.' She forced a smile. 'I know what you mean.'

SHE *DID* KNOW what he meant. And she tortured herself with it the rest of the day. Benedict thought she was an insufferable busybody. Was that how other people saw her, too? She supposed she did poke her nose into other people's business, but it was done from a genuine desire to help. Yet... wasn't that the defence of busybodies everywhere – '*I was only trying to help*?'

It was no way for a grown woman to behave.

NIALL ARRIVED home late at Gull Cottage after a victory pub crawl with his team. He made a toasted bacon sandwich and took it up to bed. She was glad he seemed to be his usual happy self, even if it was just because of the drink. As she washed up the dishes, she listened to him bumping around in the bathroom upstairs. Ever since she'd met him in the summer, she'd felt an urge to look after him. Maybe it was because he was young and she had no children of her own to worry about. She had to keep reminding herself he already had a mother. Nobody needed two.

Nelson jumped suddenly out of his basket and trotted to stand in the middle of the kitchen, ears pricked, nose twitching.

'What is it?' asked Liz. She dried her hands on a tea towel. 'Can you hear something?'

Yip! Nelson confirmed he could.

Liz cocked her head to listen. She could hear something too – a high-pitched beeping. She sniffed. And she could smell something. At first, she thought it might be Niall's toasted sandwich, but then realised it was getting stronger. With a jolt of shock she realised what the beeping noise was.

'Oh God!' For a second she was frozen on the spot; then she ran to the stairs. 'Niall!' she shouted up them. 'Niall! There's a fire in Kipper! The alarms are going off!' She grabbed her mobile and ran out onto the street, closely followed by Nelson.

From the outside, Kipper Cottage looked as tranquil and picturesque as always, but she could hear the smoke alarms beeping inside. Where were Jackie and Neville? Liz realised she'd left the house keys in Gull, so she pushed the letterbox open and peered inside. Smoke caught the back of her throat. She could see it billowing inside, lit by a flickering orange glow.

She banged on the door. 'Jackie! Neville! Are you in there?'

Nelson began to bark in earnest. Liz ran back into Gull for the keys and collided with Niall in the doorway. He was wearing only a towel and a bewildered expression.

'What the bejaysus is going on?'

'Fire! In Kipper! Nelson heard the alarms. Call the fire brigade!' She grabbed the keys and ran back out. She unlocked Kipper's door, but had to close it again quickly because of the heat and the smoke. She banged on the door, coughing.

'Neville! Jackie!' She peered through the letterbox again. This time she could see movement on the other side of the kitchen, through the smoke.

'We can't get out!' Neville's voice. Muffled and edged with fear.

'There's a window. In the storeroom!' Liz coughed.

Nelson barked.

She turned to find Niall right behind her. He'd pulled on a pair of jeans.

'Fire brigade's on the way,' he said.

'The storeroom.' Liz gasped. 'The window.'

They ran into the alley between Kipper Cottage and the smokehouse. The storeroom window was quite small, with frosted glass, but they could see movement on the other side.

'We're here!' Neville's voice came from inside. 'How do we get out?'

The window wouldn't open. Liz and Niall looked frantically around the alley.

'There!' said Liz. There was a wooden post, the remains of an old fence, leaning against the wall of the smokehouse. Niall grabbed it.

'Stand back!' he shouted.

He smashed the window with the post. Two anxious faces appeared.

'Can you climb out?' asked Liz.

'I think so,' said Neville.

'Watch the glass. There's still some in the frame.' Liz took off her jumper and put it on the windowsill to pad it. Neville and Niall helped Jackie out first. Neville climbed out gingerly after her.

'Are you both okay?' asked Liz.

'We're fine,' said Neville. He coughed. 'Just a bit shook up, is all. We were asleep when the alarms went off.'

'How bad is the fire?'

'Hard to tell. We didn't want to risk going through it.'

Then they heard sirens getting closer. Liz had never been so glad to hear anything in her life.

. . .

THE FIREMEN TOOK charge with swift efficiency. They wouldn't let anyone back into Gull in case the fire spread, so everyone stood in the street and watched the fire brigade in action. They were joined by some of their neighbours, who came out to see what was happening. Someone produced a blanket for half-naked Niall, and Liz improvised a lead for Nelson, who was getting a little overexcited.

After about half an hour or so, the firemen started to roll their hoses up again. One came over to where Liz and the others were standing.

'Who's the householder?'

'Me,' said Liz.

'You can go back in if you want. It didn't spread any farther than the front part of the kitchen. The smoke did more damage than the fire. It's going to smell for a while.'

'Do you have any idea what started it?'

'Someone pushed something through your letterbox. A firework, maybe?'

'Ruddy kids,' said Neville.

Liz frowned. Eryk and Lukasz? Surely not? She knew they were angry with her, but didn't think they would go that far. But maybe they didn't intend any real harm? Maybe they didn't expect the cottage to catch fire?

'We'll be out of your way in five minutes.' The fireman went to join the rest of his crew, to supervise their withdrawal.

Two figures squeezed past the fire engine. Kevin and Benedict.

'I heard about the call out at the station,' said Kevin anxiously. 'Is everyone alright?'

'We're all grand,' said Niall. He rubbed Nelson's ears. 'Thanks to our man here.'

Nelson grinned.

Liz met Benedict's eye and looked away. Now that she knew what he really thought of her, she didn't think she could bear his sympathy.

'I don't think you can sleep in there tonight,' she said to Neville. She felt uncomfortably close to tears.

'Don't worry about that,' said Benedict. 'There's plenty of room at my house. If you can provide bedding, Liz?'

Liz nodded.

'Congratulations.' Niall grinned at Neville and Jackie. 'You've been upgraded.'

Liz thumped him on the arm. 'Cheeky beggar.'

Everyone laughed. There was more than a tinge of relief to their laughter.

'Any idea how it started?' asked Kevin.

'A firework through the letterbox,' said Liz.

'Kids,' suggested Neville.

'Or Goths,' said Kevin. 'After one too many in the pub.'

'I don't think so.' Niall was affronted. 'That's not the kind of thing they'd do.'

'If you say so, Mrs Frankenstein.' Kevin looked sceptical.

'The lad's right,' said Neville. 'No Goth would do this.'

Kevin nodded, knowing he was outnumbered.

After the fire brigade had finished up and had reversed their engine back down Henrietta Street, Neville and Jackie went into Kipper to rescue their things. Niall settled Nelson into his basket and went upstairs. Benedict hovered in the kitchen in Gull, watching Liz sort out the bedding.

'Are we ok?' he asked at last.

'Why wouldn't we be?'

'That thing I said in the pub. It came out wrong. I don't know what's the matter with me lately.'

'Don't worry about it.'

'But I do. You're my friend, Liz. A good friend.'

Liz wanted more. She was horribly tired, and not just because of the dramatic events of the night. She was weary with carrying the burden of her secret feelings for him. Perhaps it was time to come clean? She sighed. He was looking at her intently.

'The thing is...' she began. Then she stopped. How was she going to put it?

'Yes?' prompted Benedict.

'The thing is, I...'

Neville and Jackie appeared suddenly in the doorway.

'All sorted and ready to go,' said Neville, dumping their suitcases on the floor.

Liz felt like bursting into tears. She didn't know if it was frustration or relief. She made an effort to pull herself together.

'Do you want a cuppa before you go?' she asked them.

'I don't think so.' Neville shook his head. 'We're worn out.'

'I'm really sorry about all this,' said Liz. 'I'll refund your money.'

'Don't be daft,' said Neville, genuinely appalled by the offer. 'It's hardly your fault.'

Jackie nodded. 'And it's the most exciting holiday we've ever had! First the Barghest, now this!'

Liz waved Neville, Jackie, and Benedict off in Kevin's car, then stood and stared at Kipper Cottage. She sighed. She supposed she should at least take a look inside before she locked it up for the night. Then she remembered about the storeroom window – she should really try to board it up, but just didn't have the energy. She went inside. The kitchen light didn't work because the fire brigade had turned off the electricity, so she surveyed the damage in the orange light that came through the window.

She knew she should just be happy no one was hurt, but couldn't help but feel a little sick. Smoke had blackened the walls and kitchen cabinets, and her table and chairs were charred and broken. Water lay in puddles on the stone floor, and the front of her lovely new stove had buckled with the heat.

'Thank God for insurance companies, eh?' Niall had followed her in without her realising. He was fully dressed again and had his boots on. Which was just as well, because he was standing in water.

'I know.' She nodded. 'It's just... just...' She crumpled into tears. 'It was so much hard work, Niall.'

He put his arm around her shoulders. 'It was. But we'll get it sorted again, Mrs Mac, you'll see.'

Liz wiped her eyes. She wasn't sure they would. It wasn't only the damage to the cottage but how it had happened. Someone had deliberately targeted it. Targeted *her*. Had it been Eryk and Lukasz? A prank that got out of hand? Or was it something more sinister? Philip Nethergate's henchman, warning her off his boss? Either way, it was a direct result of her meddling in Satterthwaite's murder investigation.

Benedict was right. She *was* a busybody. And she had nobody to blame for any of her trouble but herself.

20

Niall slept late the next morning, so Liz made a start tidying up Gull Cottage on her own. First she took lots of photos of the window and the smoke-damaged walls and stove for the insurance company. Then she rang several glaziers. Unfortunately, because it was Sunday, she wasn't able to find anyone who could replace the storeroom window until the following day. She boarded it up as best she could with cardboard and packing tape. Then she mopped the kitchen floor. It was so sooty; she knew it was going to take dozens of buckets of water to get it clean. Although she was daunted by the scale of the task, she was pleased to have something to keep her body occupied while she tried to make sense of the thoughts swirling inside her head.

What would have happened if she'd told Benedict how she felt about him? In the cold light of day, she was glad the drama with Neville and Jackie had stopped her. Her urge to confess had pounced on her so suddenly, due to a combination of tiredness and distress. She doubted it would have turned out well.

Benedict had such a low opinion of her. She couldn't blame him for thinking she was a busybody. She supposed she probably was. But it still hurt to know he saw her that way. She also found it astonishing that he'd thought she and Charlie Johnson were having a fling. He really didn't know her at all. She supposed she would have to talk to Gillian, as she promised she would, but she wasn't sure it was a good idea. It was hardly likely to improve her reputation as a meddler.

As she tipped the last bucket of sooty water down the sink, she pushed all thoughts of Benedict and Gillian aside and concentrated on a more pressing problem – who had started the fire? A firework through the letterbox didn't seem like the work of a professional criminal like Nethergate, and she agreed with Niall and Neville that one of the visiting Goths wasn't likely to have done it. In spite of their penchant for theatricality, Goths were generally laid-back and peace loving.

Which left Eryk and Lukasz.

After returning to Gull Cottage to shower and change, and giving Niall painkillers for his hangover, she went out again. To her surprise she saw Peggy Satterthwaite heading along Henrietta Street towards her. They stopped.

'I heard about the fire,' said Peggy. 'I thought I would come and see how you were.'

'That's very kind.'

There was an awkward pause.

'I'm so sorry about Emma,' added Liz. She wasn't sure it was the best place to offer her condolences, there in the middle of the street, but it had to be done.

Tears brimmed in Peggy's eyes. She blinked them back. 'I heard it was you who found her.'

'Yes.'

'The police... they won't tell me how she died. Did she... did she...?'

Liz jumped in to save her distress. 'I don't think she suffered in any way, Peggy. She was hit from behind. I doubt she'd have known anything about it.'

Peggy nodded. 'That's a relief.' She pulled a tissue from her pocket to dab at her eyes. 'I was so worried she might have been... frightened... or...' She tailed off again.

'I don't think so.'

'Good.' Peggy pulled herself together. 'When I think that there's someone right here, in the town, who has done something so awful, first to my poor Donnie and now to Emma, I get so... so angry!'

'I'm sure the police will catch them.'

'The police,' snorted Peggy. 'I don't suppose you saw anything when you were there?'

'Saw anything?'

'You know, anything unusual that shouldn't have been there? The police need all the help they can get.'

'No.' Liz shook her head. 'I'm sorry.'

Peggy's shoulders slumped. 'Never mind. I'm afraid I'm clutching at straws.'

'That's understandable.'

'I'll walk back to Church Street with you if you don't mind? I need to buy sweets for the trick-or-treaters. I daresay I'll have a few knocking at my door tonight. I might even buy myself a mask. Cheer myself up.'

Liz had forgotten it was Halloween.

It only took a few minutes to get to the Whitby Lolly Shop on Church Street, a delightfully old-fashioned sweet shop with jars on shelves, filled with brightly coloured candy.

'Oh, I nearly forgot,' said Peggy as she was about to go inside. 'I brought this, for your bruises.' She took a small tub

of arnica cream from her pocket and gave it to Liz. 'I
promised I would.'

'Thank you,' she said, astonished that Peggy had remembered. She put it into her own pocket and, as she did, felt
something else in there. She pulled it out.

She and Peggy looked at the flat, date-like seed in her
hand.

'I must have put it in there without realising,' said Liz,
'after I picked it up in Emma's hothouse. Do you have any
idea what it is?'

Peggy shook her head. 'I'm not much of a gardener, I'm
afraid.'

'I might plant it and see what happens. A memorial to
Emma.'

'I think she would have liked that,' said Peggy sadly.

Liz put the seed back into her pocket and left Peggy to go
into the sweet shop.

LIZ FOUND Eryk and Lukasz in the café. They were huddled
over their table, busy with cardboard, paint and glue. So busy,
in fact, that they failed to see her approaching. By the time
she was standing beside them, it was too late for them to
escape.

'Hello, you two,' she said. 'What are you making?'

Lukasz jumped and covered their project with a sheet of
cardboard. He scowled at her. 'None of your business.'

'Our Halloween costumes for tonight,' said Eryk, ignoring
his brother's glare.

'What are you going to be?' asked Liz.

Eryk looked uncertainly at his brother.

'It's a secret,' sniffed Lukasz. 'So you're the last person
we'd tell.'

Liz stared at him sombrely. 'I think we need to talk.'

'*You* can talk all you like,' said Lukasz. 'It doesn't mean *we* have to. Eh, Eryk?'

Eryk shook his head.

'Fair enough.' Liz slid onto a chair beside them. 'I'll talk. You listen. How about that?'

Lukasz shrugged.

'First of all, I'm sorry. I'm sorry I told Kevin about you being the Barghest and painting the paw print on Satterthwaite's wall. I promised I wouldn't tell anyone, and I broke that promise.'

'Yes, you did!' blurted Eryk. Lukasz remained stony.

Liz kept going. 'I did it because the only alternative would have been telling him about your mum being blackmailed, and I knew you didn't want anyone to find out about that. If I'd been able to talk to you first, and given you the choice, what would *you* have chosen?'

Eryk looked uncertain.

Lukasz wasn't convinced. 'But you told him that too, though, didn't you?' he said. 'About the letter and the list?'

'Not until much later, and only because I absolutely had to.'

'Huh.' He folded his arms.

'Kevin and the police are investigating murder, Lukasz. If I didn't tell them, someone might get away with it, and they could kill someone else.'

'Well, the police haven't caught them anyway, have they?' said Lukasz. 'And someone else *has* been murdered. That actress.'

'Mum told us about her,' said Eryk. 'It's a serious killer, she says.'

'Serial,' corrected Lukasz.

Liz smothered a smile with her hand. 'Well, it might be. We don't know for sure. The police need every scrap of information they can get to catch them.'

'Clues,' said Lukasz.

'Clues,' agreed Liz. 'So you can see why I had to tell them what I did?'

Lukasz uncrossed his arms. 'Suppose,' he muttered.

'I completely understand why you were mad at me.'

'We're still mad,' said Lukasz.

'Mad enough to put a firework through my letterbox?'

Lukasz frowned. 'What?'

'Someone put a firework through my letterbox last night. It set fire to my cottage.'

'Fire?' echoed Lukasz.

'The fire brigade had to come.'

The two boys stared at her and then at each other, lost for words. Liz watched them carefully. They were either innocent or the best actors outside Hollywood. Lukasz, as usual, was the first to find his voice.

'OMG! You think *we* did it?' It came out in an outraged squeak.

'No.' Liz realised she needed to backtrack. 'No, I don't. But I need to find out who did.'

'Is Nelson okay?' asked Eryk anxiously. 'The firework didn't scare him? He didn't burn or anything?'

Liz smiled. If she'd doubted their innocence before, she was convinced of it now. 'He's fine. In fact, he was the hero of the hour.'

Grazyna came through the curtain and spotted Liz with the boys.

'You are very quiet,' she said to the twins. 'I hope you are not bothering Mrs McLuckie?'

'We're making our costumes for tonight,' said Lukasz.

'Tonight?'

'Trick-or-treating.'

Grazyna shook her head. 'There will be no trick-or-treating tonight.'

'What?' said Lukasz, wide-eyed.

'I promised Detective Inspector Flint I would not let you go out on your own after dark. You know I have to go to Newcastle tonight.'

'Yes, but...' began Lukasz.

'Tilly and Mags will give you your tea, and you will stay with them until I get home.'

'Perhaps Tilly can take us?' suggested Eryk.

'I don't think so. She will be too busy in the café.'

'What about Niall?' said Lukasz in desperation. 'He'll do it! He has a costume too.'

Liz had to burst their bubble. 'Niall's working tonight,' she said. 'It's the Duke's busiest night of the year.'

'There has to be *someone*.' Lukasz had lost all his usual bravado. He was on the verge of tears.

'I'll do it.' The words popped out of Liz's mouth before she could really think about them.

Grazyna looked at her in astonishment. 'I cannot ask you to do it.'

'Why not?' demanded Eryk.

'Yes, why not?' echoed Lukasz.

'Because you do not like Mrs McLuckie.'

Liz almost laughed. Grazyna had many positive qualities, but tact wasn't one of them.

'We like her now,' said Lukasz.

'We do.' Eryk nodded enthusiastically. 'She's said she's sorry.'

'Sorry for what?'

'For telling the police we were the Barghest.'

'Ah.' Grazyna's frown melted. Now it made sense.

She looked at Liz. So did the boys.

'That's sorted, then,' said Liz. 'I'll pick you up here at seven thirty.' She still felt bad for betraying them to Kevin, and for thinking the worst about the fire. She was glad she'd been able to make amends so quickly.

'Thank you, Liz. That is good of you.' Grazyna spotted a vampire signalling to her from one of the tables and went to see what she wanted.

'Thanks,' said Lukasz. 'This is going to be sick!' He punched the air.

Liz nodded. She had an uneasy feeling she might have bitten off more than she could chew.

'What's your mum going to Newcastle for, anyway?' she asked, by way of a distraction.

The boys exchanged a doom-laden look. 'She's got an interview,' said Lukasz. 'She wants to leave Whitby.'

'We don't want to go,' added Eryk. 'We like it here.'

It wasn't surprising Grazyna had had enough. She probably wanted to put Satterthwaite's blackmail and the boys' adventures behind her.

'We've tried to change her mind,' said Lukasz. 'But she won't listen.'

'Perhaps she'll listen to you?' suggested his brother.

Liz shook her head. 'I doubt it.'

'It's that bloody blackmail that did it,' said Lukasz.

Liz thought she should probably correct his language, but decided not to. She wasn't his mother. She would like to help them to stay, but didn't see there was anything she could do. Perhaps there was more to Grazyna's situation than met the eye?

'Are you sure you don't know what your mum was being blackmailed about?' she asked.

The boys looked at each other, passing a silent question between them. Eryk nodded at Lukasz.

'Actually,' said Lukasz, 'we think we do.'

21

'The police are after her,' said Eryk, solemn-eyed.

'What?' That wasn't what Liz expected.

'Not here!' hissed Lukasz, casting an anxious look around the café.

She waited for the boys to tidy their things away and get their coats; then they left the Full Moon and cut down the ghaut onto the foreshore, where Liz and Nelson had outrun Nethergate's henchman a couple of days earlier.

The tide was out, so there was a bit more beach than usual. A supernaturally pale young couple were "sunbathing" on the pebbles, even though it was barely above freezing and they were dressed in huge, black overcoats. Lukasz led Liz and Eryk farther along the beach until he thought they couldn't be overheard.

'Mum's on the run,' he said.

'What makes you think that?'

'She's been acting really weird ever since the paw-print thing.'

Eryk nodded. 'Really weird. She made us hide behind the sofa!'

Lukasz elaborated. 'When the police told us to come to the police station, it wasn't the first time they'd tried to talk to us about it. They came to the flat first. Mum saw them coming, through the window. She made us hide and be quiet until they'd gone away. They got us eventually, though.'

'Mum was scared. She doesn't like the police.'

Liz supposed that was true for a lot of people, but hiding behind the sofa did seem a little extreme.

'Plus,' said Lukasz, 'we move a lot.'

'A lot!'

'This is the longest we've ever stayed anywhere.'

'Ever!'

Liz knew they'd only been in Whitby since the summer. Less than four months.

Lukasz bent to pick up a stone, and hefted it in his hand.

'And,' he said, 'we don't go to school.' He tried to skim the stone. It didn't bounce on the surface at all, but sank straight under the waves.

Liz was shocked. 'What? Never?'

'Mum teaches us at home,' said Eryk. 'At least, she tries to.'

That explained a lot, not only why they were around so much during the day, but also their unruly behaviour. Grazyna really had her hands full.

'Why doesn't she want you to go to school?'

Lukasz picked up another stone and shrugged. 'We don't know, but we don't mind. School's a pain.'

'You won't tell anyone, will you?' asked Eryk. 'We don't want her to get into trouble.'

'Of course not.' Liz was baffled. If Grazyna was trying to avoid the authorities, she wouldn't be able to register the boys in school. It looked like she was *already* in trouble. But what kind of trouble?

'Bugger,' said Lukasz. His second stone had also disappeared with a plop.

'You need a flatter one,' said Liz. She bent to choose one. 'Look. Like this.'

Lukasz peered at it.

'See? It's flat, round and smooth. And you need to throw it lower, skim it across the water.'

She demonstrated. Her stone made one... two... three skips before sinking.

'Wow,' breathed Eryk. 'You're good.'

Liz got back to the business in hand. 'Why do you think she might be trying to avoid the police?'

Lukasz shrugged.

'Maybe she robbed a bank?' suggested Eryk.

'Yeah, right,' scoffed Lukasz. 'That's why we always have beans for tea, and she has to buy our clothes in charity shops. Don't be stupid.' Lukasz's cheekbones were blotched with anger, although Liz suspected it wasn't really aimed at his brother.

'Sorry,' said Eryk.

Liz was sorry too. If Grazyna was trying to stay under the radar of the authorities – for whatever reason – she wouldn't be able to claim income support or family benefit, or get any financial help at all. As a single mother, that would be really difficult. Liz had never realised things were so hard for her. She wasn't as observant as she liked to think.

'Can you help us?' asked Lukasz. 'We want to stay in Whitby.'

'I don't know,' said Liz. 'It isn't really any of my business, is it?' She seemed to be saying that a lot lately.

'But we *need* your help,' insisted Lukasz. He glanced at his brother, who was bending over examining stones, and lowered his voice. '*I* need your help. I have to look after them.'

Liz didn't know what to say. She looked into Lukasz's pleading dark eyes... and capitulated.

'I'll try,' she said. She might be a busybody, but sometimes busybodies had their uses.

Lukasz grinned. They both turned to look at Eryk just as he launched a pebble across the surface of the water. It bounced once... two... three... four times!

'Yay!' he shouted.

'Well done!' said Liz.

'Huh,' sniffed Lukasz. 'Bet you can't do it again.'

SHE TOOK them back to the Full Moon café, then headed home to Gull Cottage. She really didn't know what to do next. Grazyna was private and fiercely proud and was likely to resist any offer of help. And what could she realistically do to help her, anyway?

She gave Nelson his lunch and took him out for a quick walk before sitting down at her laptop to fill in her insurance claim form. She didn't want to do it – she'd have to get quotations for the repairs before she could complete it properly – but she felt she should at least make a start.

She was distracted by thoughts of Grazyna. If Grazyna had been in trouble with the police, she hadn't told Tilly or Mags. Liz was pretty sure Tilly would have mentioned it to her if she had. Maybe Grazyna was worried they would find out and fire her. If that was the case, there *might* be something Liz could do about it.

She filled in her name and address on the form and then her policy number. Then she spotted Emma's seed on the table that she'd taken out of her pocket. The idea to plant it had come to her suddenly, in the middle of her conversation with Peggy, but it wasn't a bad one. She would have to find a plant pot and some compost. Emma had grown it in her hothouse. Would the cottage be warm enough? She supposed that would depend on what the seed actually was.

Fully aware she was procrastinating – avoiding the claim form – she took a photo of the seed with her phone and ran it through a plant identifier app.

When she saw the results, her eyes opened wide.

22

'What's this?' asked Kevin, staring at the small, brown object Liz had put into his hand. They were sitting in their usual shelter on the West Cliff. It was cold, their breath visible in the salty air.

'*Nux vomica.*'

'Sounds nasty.'

'It is,' Liz agreed. 'It's also known as the strychnine seed.'

Kevin put the seed down and wiped his hand on his trousers. He had a sandwich in his other hand. He looked at it and put that down too. A nearby herring gull hopped closer, eyeing it.

'It's the same as the ones in Emma Summers' conservatory,' he said.

'That's where I found it.' Liz met his look. 'I put it in my pocket without thinking.'

'You think Donnie Satterthwaite was poisoned with them?'

'I'd say it's a fair bet. It's not as if you can find strychnine lying around anywhere.'

'So Emma Summers poisoned him?'

Liz shrugged. 'We know he was blackmailing her.' Then she thought again. 'Actually, I'm not sure about that.'

'Why not?'

'The blackmail note and the list were handwritten. Donnie Satterthwaite was dyslexic. He didn't like to write anything by hand.'

'Doesn't mean he never did, though.'

'I suppose not.'

'And the boys saw him delivering it.'

'True.'

Kevin tossed his half-eaten sandwich to the herring gull. It caught it in mid-air and flapped away. He took some cling film from his lunchbox and carefully wrapped it around the seed.

'There are still more questions than answers,' said Liz.

'Questions *you* shouldn't even be asking.'

'I just want to help Grazyna and Gillian.'

Kevin nodded. 'We've spoken to them both. Grazyna denied she was being blackmailed, as you said she would, but Gillian told us about the baby. I think that's why she's broken up with Dad, isn't it?'

'I think so.'

'I don't think he would think badly of her.'

'I don't, either. But it's not our place to tell him, is it?'

'I suppose not.'

'He's asked me to talk to her,' said Liz, 'but I'm not sure what to say that I haven't already.'

'That's put you in a difficult position. I'm sorry.' Kevin knew her feelings for Benedict were stronger than friendship. She hadn't actually told him so, but he'd guessed, not long after Benedict and Gillian had started seeing each other. Unlike his father, Kevin was very good at reading people.

Liz sighed and changed the subject. 'What are you going to do with the seed now?'

He pushed it into his pocket. 'Get it to the lab, I suppose, and confirm it's the same stuff that was in the teacup. Even if it is, it doesn't really help us find the killer.'

'It's not Nethergate,' said Liz. 'At least as far as Satterthwaite's concerned. Nethergate had no idea he was the blackmailer, and so had no reason to kill him.'

'And how do you know that?'

'Because he thought *I* was.'

'What?'

Liz realised she didn't want to go into that. 'You know... we could be looking at *two* killers.'

'Great.' Kevin groaned. 'As if things aren't bad enough. And it's *me*, by the way.'

'What?' Liz's eyes opened wide.

'*I* could be looking at two killers.'

'Oh. Yes.' She laughed. 'That's what I meant.'

'Yeah, right.'

'There's also another possibility,' said Liz.

'What's that?' Kevin didn't seem particularly keen to hear the answer.

'That the murders had nothing at all to do with the blackmail. In which case, we're back to square one.' She corrected herself. '*You're* back to square one.'

'Well, thanks a lot for that,' said Kevin wryly. 'That's very helpful.' He stood up. 'I suppose I'd better get this to the lab.' He buttoned his jacket. 'What about you? Do you have plans this afternoon?'

'Not this afternoon, but tonight I'm going trick-or-treating.'

'Trick-or-treating?' Kevin raised his eyebrows. 'With the boys?'

She nodded.

Kevin smirked. As she looked at him, his smirk expanded into a smile and then a laugh – a full-on, genuine belly laugh.

'What's so funny?'

Kevin wiped his eyes. 'Nothing.' But he was still grinning when he left her. 'Have fun!'

She watched him get into his car in the Pavilion Drive car park.

Actually, now that she thought about it, she *did* have something to do that afternoon. She had to catch Grazyna before she left for Newcastle.

SHE ONLY JUST MADE IT. She found her in the café kitchen with her coat on, giving last minute instructions to Tilly and Mags.

'I have put the batter mix for the puddings in the fridge, and the new order from the cash and carry in the storeroom.' She gave Tilly a packet of pills. 'Eryk has to take these after he eats at teatime. They are for his allergies. And remember, Lukasz will not eat eggs. They make him shit.'

Liz grinned. The finer nuances of English vocabulary were still something of a challenge to Grazyna.

Tilly threw up her hands in mock horror. 'No eggs!'

Mags gave her a quelling look. 'What time do you think you'll be back?' she asked Grazyna.

'Not until late. My interview isn't until six thirty.'

'I still don't understand why you're going,' said Mags. 'You have a perfectly good job here.'

'My mind is made up.' Grazyna turned, businesslike, to Liz. 'Please do not let the boys eat too much candy, or I will never get them to sleep tonight.'

'Okay.'

Grazyna fastened her coat. Liz realised she had to work fast. She saw the soup bubbling on the stove and moved closer to it.

'Something smells good,' she said.

'Pumpkin soup,' said Tilly.

'Mmm.' Liz steeled herself. There was no elegant way of doing this. 'Much better than prison food, eh, Tills?'

Tilly stared at her as if her head had exploded. Liz felt laughter bubble up at her reaction, but managed to push it down again. She wasn't worried about offending Tilly and Mags by mentioning prison. They made no secret of the time they'd spent there.

But Grazyna obviously didn't know. She stared at Tilly. 'Prison food?'

Mags and Tilly shared a look. 'Not something we care to remember.'

'I can imagine.' Grazyna considered them both and then looked hard at Liz. Liz supposed she hadn't been very subtle.

'I must go now, to the station,' said Grazyna. 'You will come with me, Liz.' It was a command, not a request. They left Tilly and Mags staring at each other – what the hell was that about?

It was getting dark outside. 'We will walk and talk, to the station.'

'If you like.' Liz wrapped her coat more firmly around her. The air was cold and damp. It felt like rain. Grazyna strode off at a blistering pace. Liz hurried to keep up.

'You had a purpose, I suppose, in mentioning prison?'

'I think you know I did.'

'I have not been to prison.' She glanced sideways at Liz. 'But I do not want to go there.'

'Is there any danger of that?'

Grazyna said nothing.

'Is that why you were being blackmailed?'

Grazyna still said nothing, but continued her march to the station.

Liz tried again. 'I know that you hide from the police. I

know the boys don't go to school.' She caught Grazyna's arm to bring her to a halt. 'I want to help you, if I can.'

She saw some of the tension leave the other woman's shoulders.

'If I tell you, Liz, you promise to say nothing?'

'Of course.'

Grazyna nodded. 'Then let us talk properly. At the station.'

The town's railway station was only a minute's walk away, a small Victorian building with just two platforms. When they got there, they saw on the board that Grazyna's train was running five minutes late. The rain had started – an insistent patter of raindrops, ripe with the promise of harder rain to come. They took shelter under the platform canopy, and Liz waited patiently for Grazyna to begin. When she did, it was from an unexpected direction.

'I am not Polish,' she said. She nodded at Liz's surprise. 'I never told anyone I was. It is just a presumption people make, and I am happy not to correct them. I am from Belarus. You know Belarus?'

Liz shook her head, ashamed that she knew nothing about it.

'It is a beautiful country.' Grazyna's habitually stern expression softened. But... difficult. We have had many problems there. I will not try to explain the politics, it would take too long... When the boys were eighteen months old, my husband was arrested. I was warned by friends to leave the country. We had no passports, no papers, but we managed to make it into Poland. We went from Poland by sea to Denmark and then to Amsterdam and then by fishing trawler to Grimsby. All without papers.'

Liz said nothing, stunned into silence by the scale of Grazyna's struggles and the strength it must have taken for her to get to England alone, illegally, with two babies.

'I found a job in Grimsby and took the decision not to turn myself in to the authorities. I cannot risk being sent back to Belarus, Liz.'

'What about your husband?'

Grazyna shrugged. 'He is dead, I think.'

'The boys don't know any of this?'

'I will tell them when they are older, but for now I cannot risk them giving us away accidentally. Also...' Grazyna paused. 'I want them to have a childhood without such a burden.' She gave Liz a searching look. 'I have already been interviewed once by the police. You see now why I cannot risk coming to their attention again?'

Liz nodded. 'I'm sorry.'

'It is not your fault. What is this with the English that they insist on apologising for things that have nothing to do with them?'

Liz supposed that was true, but had no answer.

'Isn't there any way I can persuade you to stay in Whitby?' she asked instead. 'Satterthwaite's dead. He can't threaten you anymore.'

'Even so, it is better we move on, I think. The boys do not behave themselves, and we are too much the target of gossip – and Detective Inspector Flint. However... I must admit that I have enjoyed it here.'

'We'll miss you. And Lukasz and Eryk.'

'They are not wicked. Just restless.'

'I know.'

Grazyna stood up and turned away. Liz suspected she was trying to wipe her eyes without her seeing. 'This is my train.'

The train pulled onto the platform. Grazyna jumped on board as soon as the doors had opened.

'Look after my boys tonight!' she called through the window. 'And remember – not too much candy!'

23

Grazyna had given Liz a lot to think about. Who could have guessed what she'd been through? What she was *still* going through. Liz was curious to know how Satterthwaite had found out about her being in the country illegally, and how he'd known about Gillian's baby. She supposed that, as a journalist, he'd had mad investigative skills.

'Is everything okay, Mrs Mac?' asked Niall. 'You're miles away.'

'Sorry. I suppose I was.' She joined him at the table to eat the Bolognese she'd made for them both. He didn't launch into it, as he usually did, but toyed with his spaghetti. Not like him. Liz was worried.

'How're things with you?' she asked.

'Just tired. I won't be sorry when the festival's over. Then I can start helping you put Kipper right again.'

'What about your contract in Liverpool?'

'Ah... that won't be happening.'

'Why not?'

He shook his head. 'Is it okay if we don't talk about it? It's a sore point right now.'

Liz thought about persisting, but decided against it. She nodded.

He continued to push the Bolognese around his plate. 'What time are you going out trick-or-treating tonight?'

'About half seven.'

'What are the boys going as?'

'I'm not sure. Their costumes are made from cardboard.'

Niall was alarmed. 'Is that a good idea? The forecast's terrible.'

'Don't worry,' she said. 'I have a plan B.'

The same thing had occurred to Liz too. After she'd put Grazyna on the train, she'd stopped off in Baxtergate to buy two masks. Not as inventive as homemade costumes, but a whole lot better than a pile of sodden cardboard and dribbling poster paint.

'Will you be wearing your costume to work tonight?' she asked him.

'I will. The Bride of Frankenstein will be making her final appearance. I'm going to miss her.'

'You like wearing a dress?'

'I do. It's very... liberating. Perhaps I should wear one more often. My ma always wanted a daughter.' He grinned – a flash of his old self. 'Will Nelson be alright tonight on his own?'

'I should think so. I can't imagine I'll be out more than an hour or two.'

Niall raised his eyebrows. 'When there's Eryk and Lukasz and sweets involved? Are you sure about that?'

Liz pulled a face. 'You might have a point.'

'Well, if it does take longer, text me, and I'll give Nelson a leg stretch when I'm on my break. I usually take a break around nine thirty.'

'I will. Thanks.'

His face grew serious. 'I do appreciate it, you know. Everything you do for me.'

'Well, the feeling's mutual. You do a lot for me too.'

He thought about that. 'That's true, right enough,' he said. Then he winked.

LIZ WAS LATE LEAVING the house. She'd been waiting for a break in the rain, but it never came. It continued to pour down, a biblical torrent, making the gutters run with water. Eventually she realised she couldn't delay any longer. The deluge wasn't likely to stop Eryk and Lukasz. She zipped up her coat and went out. She hurried, head down, along Henrietta Street. Not surprisingly, there was no one else around. Rain swept across the cobbles and blew into her face, stinging her cheeks. As she hurried past the bottom of the abbey steps, she glanced up, towards the church.

And stopped.

There was something on the steps. A black shape, about a third of the way up. She wiped the rain from her eyes to see more clearly. Whatever it was had a rough, shaggy coat and four legs. It was hard to tell how big it was, because there was nothing beside it she could use for scale. It looked as if it had been on its way up the steps, but now had stopped. As she watched, it turned its head and glared at her with yellow eyes. A chill rushed through her, turning her legs to jelly. Her hands went numb, and her bag hit the ground. She couldn't breathe. Couldn't move.

Finally, she broke eye contact. She bent to pick up her bag. When she straightened up again, the creature had gone.

It took her a few moments to realise what had happened. Had she just seen the Barghest?

· · ·

'No way!' breathed Eryk. He was thrilled.

'I TOLD YOU!' shouted Iris. 'BUT YOU DIDN'T BELIEVE ME, DID YOU?'

'I'm sorry, Iris. I have to admit I thought you'd imagined it, but now...' Liz shook her head, still in shock.

The old lady drained her bottle of lager and nodded with satisfaction. 'JUST LIKE I SAID. YELLOW EYES! I SAID THAT, IRWIN, DIDN'T I?'

'You did,' agreed her long-suffering son. 'Among many, many other things.'

The café was unusually quiet; the rain was keeping most people indoors. The only other customers were two bedraggled steampunk ladies trying not to make it obvious they were listening to the conversation.

'Tell us again,' pleaded Lukasz. 'Was it very scary?'

'Very,' said Liz. 'I thought my heart had stopped.'

'EXACTLY WHAT HAPPENED TO ME!'

Tilly gave Liz a mug. 'Get that down you,' she said. It was black coffee laced with brandy, so strong it made Liz gasp.

'Is someone else going to die now?' asked Eryk.

'No,' said Irwin.

'DEFINITELY!' bellowed Iris.

'Aren't you going to take that wet coat off?' Tilly asked Liz. 'You're soaked through.'

'There's no point,' said Liz, 'if I'm going out again.'

'Surely you're not going back out?' Tilly was appalled. Eryk and Lukasz both snapped to attention, like spiky-headed meerkats.

'You promised!' squeaked Lukasz.

Liz exchanged a helpless look with Tilly and shrugged.

'Well, at least take that wet top off,' said Tilly. 'I'll get you a T-shirt. I think we might have one left out the back.'

'You've sold them all?' Liz was amazed. 'You had hundreds.'

'Just about everyone in town has one,' said Irwin. He pulled his jacket open to reveal his own Barghest T-shirt. 'And all the visitors.'

'I've made a bit of a killing,' admitted Tilly, with a grin.

'*There is a tide in the affairs of men which, taken at the flood, leads on to fortune,*' quoted Irwin.

'Exactly!' said Tilly.

'Talking of floods, I think it's easing off.' Mags was peering out the window.

'Yay! Come on, Eryk. Let's get our costumes on!' The twins ran out through the curtain and thumped up the stairs to the flat.

Tilly found Liz the last Barghest T-shirt, and Liz changed into it in the kitchen. She didn't really want to go outside again, but knew there was no way she could wriggle out of it. The boys weren't going to let her break another promise.

After a few minutes, they thumped back down the stairs and burst through the beaded curtain.

'Ta-dah!' yelled Lukasz. Their faces were painted green, and they were naked except for two large cardboard boxes that hung from straps on their shoulders.

'WHAT THE DEVIL ARE YOU SUPPOSED TO BE?' bellowed Iris.

'Can't you tell?' asked Eryk, dismayed. Everyone just looked at them.

'Look,' said Lukasz. The word BOXTROLL had been painted on the side of both boxes.

'Boxtroll?' said Liz.

'Yeah. They're like goblins that live underground and wear boxes instead of clothes.'

'Everyone thinks they're wicked,' added Eryk, 'but they're not.'

Liz could see a certain parallel there. Tilly frowned at the boxes that had been recycled from her cash-and-carry delivery.

'I hope you're wearing something under there. You'll catch your deaths.'

'We have our pants on.'

Liz shook her head. 'It's freezing. Go back upstairs and put something on underneath.'

'But it'll spoil the costumes!' protested Lukasz.

'It won't. Everyone will still know what you are.' Liz met Lukasz's glare with an equally stubborn look of her own. 'I mean it. I'm not parading you through the town naked. Your mother would never forgive me.'

They disappeared again and reappeared two minutes later, wearing jeans and their Barghest T-shirts under the boxes.

'That's better,' said Liz.

But Tilly wasn't convinced. 'Aren't those boxes going to get awfully wet?'

Lukasz lifted his chin. 'They'll be fine!'

THEY LASTED LESS than fifteen minutes in the rain. Even though it was nowhere near as bad as it had been, it was still a persistent drizzle. Liz and the boys only managed to make a couple of house calls before it had soaked right through the cardboard, and the boxes hung shapelessly from the straps on the boys' shoulders. Liz knew it wouldn't be long before they disintegrated completely.

'We can't keep going like this,' said Lukasz. 'We look rubbish.'

Eryk peered into his trick-or-treat bucket. 'We've hardly got anything yet!' He thrust his bucket at Liz. He only had a fudge finger, a packet of wine gums and a satsuma in it.

Liz looked at their tragic faces streaked with green poster paint.

'Come on,' she said. 'We're not going to let a bit of water get the better of us, are we?'

She shepherded them into a shop doorway and helped them strip the boxes off. She pushed the sodden card into a nearby wheelie bin and wiped their faces with a tissue she had in her pocket. It was as wet as everything else, but she managed to get most of the green paint off with it.

'But we're not dressed up now,' protested Lukasz. 'No one will give us anything.'

Liz grinned. 'I've thought of that.' She fished the masks out of her bag and gave them to them. 'Ta-dah!'

'Werewolves!' breathed Eryk.

'Cool!'

They put the masks on and grinned at each other. Eryk tipped his head back and howled. It was very loud and very convincing. Liz shivered. Given her experience earlier in the evening, she'd rather he hadn't done that.

'Shh! No howling!'

'But I like howling,' said Eryk.

'So do I,' said Lukasz.

'You don't want to get in trouble with DI Flint again, do you?'

The boys exchanged a look. They really didn't. But they recovered quickly.

'Let's do White Horse Yard next!' said Lukasz. They scurried off. Liz hurried to catch up with them.

THE EVENING WENT MORE SMOOTHLY after that. Because of the rain, there were more people at home than outdoors, and the boys managed to collect quite a haul of chocolate and sweets.

Lukasz was disappointed that not a single person chose trick rather than treat – he had an egg in his bucket, just in case – but even he had to admit that people were very generous.

When they reached the edge of Pannet Park, Liz decided to call it a night.

'We should be heading back.'

'We can't stop now,' said Lukas. 'These are the good houses.'

He had a point. Pannet Park was the posh part of town. Liz wasn't sure that wealthier people were necessarily more generous than anyone else, but she agreed to keep going for a little while longer, just in case. They called at Benedict's first, but he was out. He'd left a small selection of sweets behind the jack-o'-lantern on his porch. Liz had to persuade the boys not to take it all, in case someone called later. After that, they tried another couple of houses that had their lights on. No one answered the door of either of them.

'There's someone in there,' said Lukasz, on the step of the second one. 'I can hear them moving about.' He took out his egg. 'Can I throw it?'

Liz hesitated.

'Go on. Please. I only brought one, and I don't want to carry it all the way home again.'

Liz had definitely seen a curtain twitch.

'Go on, then.'

The egg splattered on the door, and they made a run for it. Liz didn't feel too bad – she knew the rain would wash the worst of it off.

'We really do have to go home now,' she said when she'd got her breath back on the street. She was so cold that she didn't think she'd ever be warm again.

'One more house,' begged Lukasz.

'Just one. Please.'

She was about to put her foot down, but then remembered somewhere nearby where they were guaranteed a treat or two. 'Okay. But this is definitely the last one.'

Peggy was ready for visitors. A pair of carved pumpkins grinned out at them from the two windows that flanked the front door, and the bay trees on the porch were draped in cobwebs that had somehow survived the rain. A sign on the door, held up by a slightly soggy cardboard skeleton, said:

Abandon hope all ye who enter here!

Lukasz nodded approvingly. 'Spooky.'

Liz rang the doorbell.

The boys adjusted their masks.

'Are you sure we can't howl?'

'No howling.'

'Not even one little one?'

'No.'

The door opened... and Liz recoiled. A red-lipped clown leered at them from the step. Liz gasped and staggered back.

Peggy took off her mask. 'Are you okay, Mrs McLuckie?'

'Yes... yes... I'm sorry.' Liz bent over, gulping air.

'I didn't mean to scare you,' said Peggy. 'Well, I did... but not that much.'

The twins took off their own masks and grinned. Who knew Liz was such a wuss?

'I just... I have a thing about clowns. Can I... can I sit down for a minute?'

'Of course, come in. Come in all of you.'

Peggy ushered them into the hall and showed Liz to a chair.

'I'll be fine in a minute.' Liz took deep breaths and tried to calm her thumping heart.

Peggy offered a bowl of sweets to Eryk and Lukasz.

'I'm so glad you came,' she said. 'I have heaps left.'

The boys both took a fistful of candy from the bowl. Lukasz saw Liz's warning look and put some of it back.

'Don't be silly,' said Peggy. 'Take as much as you want. I'll never eat it all.'

Sweat prickled on Liz's forehead, and she felt sick. She tried to keep her eyes averted from the mask Peggy had put on the hall table, but they kept creeping back to it. It held a horrible fascination for her.

Peggy took in their appearance. 'Goodness! Look at the three of you. You're soaking wet.' She put a hand to Eryk's forehead. 'And so cold! I was just making cocoa downstairs, if you'd like some?'

'Yeah!'

'Yes, please!'

Liz nodded. She just wanted to get away from that bloody mask. She'd be glad to warm up a bit, too. And maybe afterwards they could go out the back door rather than having to come past the mask again?

Peggy's kitchen was in the basement. They followed her down the stairs, into a low-ceilinged room with expensive kitchen units painted a tasteful shade of grey. The room wasn't drab, however. There were several movie posters framed on the walls, in 1950s candy colours: *Whatever Happened to Baby Jane*, *Mildred Pierce*, *The Women*. One face was common to all of them.

'Is cocoa okay,' asked Peggy, 'or would you prefer eggnog?'

'I can't eat eggs...' began Lukasz.

Liz couldn't prevent what she knew was coming next.

'... they make me shit.'

Peggy's periwinkle eyes opened wide.

'Sorry,' said Liz. She glared at Lukasz.

He shrugged. 'They do!'

'Cocoa it is, then,' said Peggy. Her tone had changed slightly; the language had clearly upset her. 'It shouldn't take too long.' She looked at Liz. 'Would you mind getting some milk out of the fridge? It's in the door.'

Liz went to the old-fashioned American fridge. There was a sheet of green notepaper pinned to it with a magnet – *butter, washing-up liquid, bin bags* – the beginnings of a shopping list. Liz stared. She recognised that handwriting and the notepaper!

Doing her best not to betray her shock, she found the carton of milk in the fridge and took it to the range, where Peggy was busy with a saucepan and mugs. The boys had taken a seat at the table and were staring around the room, impatient for cocoa.

'Oh!' Liz looked pointedly at her watch. 'I've just remembered. I need to ask Niall to walk Nelson for me. Excuse me a minute.' She turned away and took her phone from her pocket, to text Niall.

You there?

For a moment or two there was nothing; then, to her relief, she saw he was typing his reply.

About to take my break. Want me to walk Nelson?

Call Kevin. Tell him to come to Peggy Satterthwaite's NOW. BRING HELP!

She sent her message, then put her phone away. She could have texted Kevin directly, but hadn't wanted to risk him not picking it up. She knew Niall would get through to him.

'Sorry about that.' She smiled at Peggy and put away her

phone. Peggy smiled back at her with a sweet smile, but Liz wasn't fooled.

'I was admiring your movie posters,' Liz said. 'You're a big movie fan?'

'I am. Joan Crawford is my favourite, as you can probably tell.'

'A great actress. Not such a great mother, though.'

Peggy frowned. 'I'm not sure you should believe everything you read.'

'What was her daughter's biography called again?' Liz knew perfectly well but wanted Peggy to say it.

'*Mommie Dearest.*'

'Was that Donnie's nickname for you, by any chance?'

Peggy's brows rose. 'How did you guess? It was just his bit of fun. He didn't mean anything bad by it.'

Mommie Dearest. MD. But that wasn't the real clincher. The real clincher was the list on the fridge door. The same green notepaper as the blackmail list. The same handwriting.

Liz watched as Peggy put the milk on to heat, feeling more and more uncomfortable about being there. Was she putting the boys in danger?

'You know what?' she said. 'I think we'd better pass on the cocoa after all. I promised their mum I'd get them home for ten o'clock.'

The twins glared at her. *What?*

'When did you do that?' said Lukasz.

Liz tried to stare him down.

'Oh, that's a pity,' said Peggy, 'when I've already started making it. Are you sure?'

'Sorry, yes.' She didn't want to eat or drink anything in Peggy's house.

Peggy nodded. 'Best not upset their mum, eh? Mother knows best.' She handed the milk carton back to Liz. 'Can you put this back, please?'

Liz took the milk to the fridge and risked another look at the list. It was definitely the...

Then everything exploded into stars.

24

'What did you do that for?' Lukasz's distressed voice sounded a long way away.

Liz tried and failed to open her eyes. She could feel the floor, unyielding beneath her, but everything else was a mush of pain.

'Because I don't like nosy parkers.' Peggy's voice was closer, laced with menace. 'I don't like foul-mouthed little boys, either. I should wash your mouth out with soap.'

'Run, Eryk!'

Liz heard them go. Heard their feet pounding up the stairs, with a lighter tread – Peggy's – following.

With a supreme effort, Liz pushed herself up off the floor. Nothing would stay still – not the floor, the walls or even her own feet. Everything kept lurching away from her. She put a hand to the back of her head, and it came away red and sticky. She couldn't believe she'd turned her back on a double murderer. What an idiot!

She reeled out of the kitchen and followed them up the stairs as fast as she could, swallowing back nausea. When she got to the top, she saw Eryk and Lukasz had reached the front door. They were rattling the door handle.

'It's locked,' gasped Lukasz.

'I have the key.' Peggy stood in the middle of the hall, with her hands on her hips. 'You'll not get out that way.'

Lukasz's eyes darted around in desperation, then settled on one solution.

'Upstairs. Quick!' The boys ran for the stairs.

Liz bit back frustration. If the boys had tried to rush Peggy together, they would probably have been able to subdue her. But they were just ten years old. Peggy was an adult. The thought probably never occurred to them. Now they were trapped upstairs, in a house that was unfamiliar.

Peggy had the advantage.

'Leave them alone!' Liz shouted.

Peggy turned to face her, masking her surprise. 'Still alive, are we? I suppose you are younger than Emma. Tougher. Poor Emma was always a bit of a wet lettuce.'

'That was *your* cardigan I saw in the hothouse. The pink one.'

'I only realised I'd left it there later. I wondered if you'd recognised it.'

Liz remembered Peggy grilling her about what she'd seen at the crime scene.

'Emma was your friend. Why would you kill her?'

'Because she caught me stealing more *Nux vomica*. I'd used all I had on Donnie, and thought some more might come in handy. She saw me taking it and put two and two together. She tried to hide it, but I could tell. I saw it on her face, the second it dawned on her. The same shock I saw on yours.'

Liz was feeling stronger now.

'The police are on their way. Give it up, Peggy. It's over.'

Peggy shook her head. 'I don't think so. Not just yet.'

She reached for the hall table and put on her mask.

Fear sluiced through Liz, white-hot and paralysing. She staggered back.

'You don't like clowns?' Peggy jeered, her voice filtered through the plastic. 'I think they're lovely.' She advanced on Liz. 'So much fun.'

Liz retreated. She couldn't think straight. All she could think about, all she could see, was that awful face coming towards her. She covered her eyes, overcome with horror. She heard breathing in front of her and a low chuckle. Then someone pushed her hard in the chest.

A chasm yawned behind her. She tumbled backwards down the stairs.

Except... she didn't. Not all the way.

She lay on her back at an odd angle, winded. It took her a moment to get her breath back, and to realise what had broken her fall – her right foot had caught on one of the banisters about halfway down the stairs. It really, really hurt, but at least she was still alive. And conscious. She could hear someone running on the floor above her. Peggy had turned her attention to the boys, thinking Liz was done with.

But she wasn't. Not by a long shot.

She pulled her foot out of the banister rail and stood up. She put her weight on it experimentally and winced from the pain. Her head was hurting, too, but she had to move. She climbed the basement stairs again, ignoring the throb in her injured foot.

There was no one in the hall. Liz averted her eyes from the hideous clown mask on the floor. She could see the strobe of a blue light through the hall windows and heard a car door slam.

Kevin with the cavalry.

She hesitated, wondering what to do. Peggy had the key to the door, so she couldn't let Kevin in. She could try to help him force it, but who knew how long that would take? A *crash* from upstairs made up her mind. The boys needed her.

She hobbled up the stairs as fast as her sore foot and pounding head would let her. There was no sign of anyone on the first-floor landing. A vase had been knocked off a table. There was spilt water and scattered roses on the carpet. Liz kept going, hobbling up the next flight to the second floor.

Another *crash*.

'Leave us alone!' Lukasz's voice. Distant. Somewhere at the top of the house.

Liz hurried up another two floors as fast as she could. On the topmost landing she saw a door open. Stairs to the attic.

'Don't come any closer!' Lukasz's voice was frantic.

'Or what? What are you going to do?' Peggy was calm, her tone reasonable. Somehow that made it worse.

Liz crept up the wooden stairs and winced when one creaked under her foot. She paused. Had Peggy heard?

'Go on,' said Peggy. 'Jump if you like. See if I care.'

Liz peered over the top of the last stair, into the attic. It ran the length of the house, with two dormer windows. Lukasz and Eryk had managed to open one, and were perched on the windowsill. Peggy had her back to Liz.

Liz did a quick calculation. Her heart thumped. They were four floors up!

Peggy advanced on the boys. Lukasz and Eryk each put one leg out the window. They clung to each other.

'We can do it,' Lukasz said to his brother. 'She can't get us on the roof.'

Dear God! The rain was still falling. Liz could hear it on the tiles. It would only take one little slip, and they'd be done for. How would she explain that to Grazyna?

She looked around for a weapon. The attic was stacked with boxes and junk – broken furniture, books, and vinyl records. Liz spotted a bag of golf clubs within grabbing range.

Thump, thump followed by a *crash* from downstairs.

Peggy whirled round. Liz ducked out of sight just in time.

'The police!' gasped Lukasz.

'Too late for you,' said Peggy.

Liz peeked out from behind the boxes.

Peggy was advancing on the boys, trying to drive them out the window. Liz rose stealthily from her hiding place and grabbed one of the golf clubs.

Lukasz's attention was out of the window, his face fierce with concentration. He swung his other leg out over the sill. But Eryk was looking at Peggy. He spotted Liz over Peggy's shoulder. His eyes widened. Liz put her finger to her lips.

'You're a horrible old witch!' Eryk yelled.

Peggy sneered. 'I'm glad you're not my little boy. If you were, I would teach you some manners.'

Lukasz slipped, with a yell. Eryk made a grab for him.

Peggy lunged forward, but Liz was faster. She clouted the old lady over the head with the club. Peggy crumpled. Liz scrambled over her and ran to the boys. She reached them just as Lukasz slipped from Eryk's grasp. She grabbed the front of his T-shirt and managed to haul him back in through the window. They all fell in a heap on the floor.

'Phew,' said Lukasz when they'd got their breath back. 'That was a bit close.' His face was chalk-white. Liz hugged him. Then Eryk.

'You little stars!' she said.

The boys hugged each other.

Peggy groaned.

Eryk startled. 'She's awake!'

'Sit on her!' urged Liz. 'Sit on her, both of you. Don't let her move!'

The boys did as they were told. Liz examined the wound on the back of her head with careful fingers. It was still bleeding. They heard several pairs of feet pounding up through the house. Eventually, a scowling face appeared at the top of the stairs.

DI Flint took in the scene – the two boys sitting on the old lady, and Liz standing over them, her hands covered in blood.

'What the hell is going on?'

'YOU WERE RIGHT.' Kevin joined Liz where she sat on the step of one of the ambulances, her foot strapped and an ice pack pressed to the back of her head. The boys were being checked over at another ambulance nearby. 'We found evidence in her study. Files on people. Compromising photos. We think she got most of it from Donnie. She has a list of all his passwords. We also found her old social work files – that's what she did before she retired.'

'You think that's how she found out about Gillian?'

'Probably.' He hesitated. 'We also found blackmail notes she'd written but hadn't sent yet. There's one addressed to Niall.'

'Niall?'

'Reminding him about the lies on his CV, and demanding more money.'

'*More* money? So she'd blackmailed him before? When did it start, do you think?'

'Sometime after Donnie's death, I'd say.'

That explained a lot – why Niall had been working so hard, why he'd turned down the job in Liverpool, and his recent, uncharacteristic bad mood. A bad mood that had started *after* Donnie had died. It was horribly ironic. Liz already knew about his fudged CV – he'd told her about it in the summer – but if he'd confided to her about the blackmail too, she would have realised Donnie couldn't possibly have been the blackmailer. Everything might have been solved a whole lot faster.

'We also found more of those strychnine seeds,' said Kevin. 'I don't think we'll have any problem making a case against her.'

'Good!'

Peggy had already been examined by the paramedics and pronounced fit to be taken to the station by DI Flint and Constable Williams.

Liz had another thought. 'When the boys saw Satterthwaite, he must have been trying to *retrieve* the letter from their post box.'

'He found out about Peggy's schemes?'

'Which was why she poisoned him.' Liz shuddered. 'Poor Donnie. What a terrible time he must have had with her.' *Mommie Dearest.*

'I still don't understand why she would blackmail people. She was hardly short of a bob or two,' said Kevin.

'From what I've seen, she's a classic narcissist. I suppose it made her feel powerful.'

'Why did she kill Emma?' asked Kevin.

'Because she saw her taking more *Nux vomica*. She told me. She was no friend to Emma. She was blackmailing her too. I daresay you'll find out why.'

There were a few dots still to be joined, but the picture was more or less clear. The rest would fall into place at some point.

'Lukasz! Eryk!' Grazyna pushed her way through the milling policemen to the boys in the ambulance.

'Mum!' They jumped out to hug her.

Over their heads, her eyes found Liz's.

Liz winced.

'Excuse me,' she said to Kevin. 'I have some explaining to do.'

25

L iz looked up at the sky. It was solid grey, pressing down on the town like a sullen blanket. Perhaps they were going to get the first snow of the season? It was certainly cold enough, a bitter, nipping cold that had arrived with the wind, straight across the North Sea from Scandinavia. Liz shivered and continued her way along Church Street.

With only a few weeks to go until Christmas, most of the shops were brightly lit, decorated with fairy lights and tinsel. The council had also put up their decorations – pretty strings of lights festooned along the main shopping streets, and an impressive tree in the market square. Liz's fellow pedestrians were almost all locals – there were very few holidaymakers at that time of year, and no Goths, vampires or monsters. They wouldn't be back for another year.

Liz heaved the tin of emulsion she was carrying into her other hand. She was beginning to wish she'd let Benedict drive her to the DIY store to get it, as he'd offered. But she'd insisted on getting it herself, because her foot was much better, and she needed to keep it moving. But the paint was heavier than she'd thought, and seemed to get heavier with every step.

As she passed the bakers, the door opened, and someone stepped out less than ten feet away from her.

'Dora Spackle!'

Dora's eyes opened wide, and she looked as if she might duck back inside the shop.

'You've been avoiding me,' said Liz. It was true. Ever since Peggy Satterthwaite had been arrested, Dora had been conspicuous by her absence. It was as if she'd suddenly winked out of existence. Liz thought she'd spotted her on Baxtergate once and had hurried to catch up with her. But Dora had obviously spotted her too, and she'd turned quickly down another street. When Liz had reached the junction, Dora had gone. She could move quickly for a woman in advanced middle age.

'Avoiding you? I don't know what you mean.' Dora stowed her loaf of bread into her old-fashioned shopping trolley and wheeled it around Liz. Then she stomped off up Church Street, towards the abbey.

Liz fell into step beside her.

'I think you do,' insisted Liz. 'I think you know I've been wanting to talk to you.'

'I can't imagine why.'

'Because there's only one other person who knew that Niall had lied about his degree on his CV. You told Peggy, didn't you?'

'I have no idea what you're talking about.'

'Did you know she was blackmailing people?'

Dora stopped, indignant. 'Of course not! What do you think I am?'

'So why did you tell her?'

'Because she was curious about him.' Dora set off again.

'Was she curious about me, too? Was that why you were following me?'

Dora cast her a sideways look.

'Don't try to deny it.'

'I wasn't about to.'

'So?'

'Peggy asked me to keep an eye on you. And before you ask me why, I have no idea. It's just as well she did, though, isn't it, or you would have been squashed by that van!'

That was true.

They'd reached the bottom of the abbey steps. Dora stomped off and started to push her shopping trolley up the donkey path that ran up the hill beside the steps. She didn't say goodbye.

Liz stared after her. As unpleasant as Dora could be, Liz still felt some sympathy. She suspected that Peggy and Emma had been her only friends, but Peggy had just been using Dora to gather information about her victims. Dora hadn't married, and Liz had no idea if she had any extended family. If not, she was going to have a very lonely Christmas.

As you sow so shall you reap.

The Bible phrase made Liz think about Gillian. Liz had tried to talk to her, as she'd promised Benedict she would, but Gillian had brushed her off – kindly, but very firmly. Benedict still had no idea what was really behind the break-up, and if Gillian didn't decide to tell him, he never would. Liz and Kevin had agreed not to say anything to him.

Liz realised with some surprise that she'd made it to Kipper Cottage. She let herself in.

Yip! Nelson greeted her with a wag of his stumpy tail, then retreated back to the safety of his basket. He had a splodge of paint on his nose.

'Here she is, at last!' cried Tilly.

'You should have let me drive you,' said Benedict. He took

the paint from Liz and gave it to Niall, who was waiting to open it.

'I need only the smallest amount,' said Grazyna.

'I need quite a bit,' said Kevin. 'Don't spill it.'

'Then stop jostling! Jaysus!'

Niall divided the emulsion between the plastic paint kettles of his friends. They were all dressed in paint-splashed clothes, except for Iris, who had wrapped herself in a length of plastic sheeting for protection and had enthroned herself in a chair with a mug of tea. As Liz looked at them, a wave of gratitude swept over her, making her eyes prickle. She made a show of taking her coat off to hide it.

'THAT NEEDS DOING AGAIN.' Iris pointed at the ceiling near the door. 'THE SOOT'S STILL SHOWING THROUGH.'

'I'll get it.' Tilly picked up the steps and hauled them to the offending spot.

Nethergate's henchman Derek had admitted to causing the fire at the cottage. He'd pushed a Catherine wheel through her letterbox as punishment for her ill-tempered conversation with Nethergate at the football match. The police had been delighted when proof of Nethergate's many criminal activities had come to light in Peggy's papers and Donnie's files – they'd been trying to pin something on him for years. After that, Derek had turned evidence against his boss, confessing not only to the fire, but a host of other misdemeanours that included pushing Liz into the road and filling the Crab and Cockle with rats in retaliation for Marty Davidson's refusal to pay protection. Nethergate was likely to go to prison for quite some time.

Charlie Johnson had also been arrested and charged with embezzlement and taking bribes. Tilly, Marty Davidson and several other licensees in the town had been let off with warnings for paying Johnson for their drinks licences.

'Anyone want a cup of tea?' asked Liz, filling the kettle at the tap.

'We have just had one,' said Grazyna.

'I'M AWASH WITH THE STUFF. MY BACK TEETH ARE FLOATING,' yelled Iris. 'I'LL HAVE TO HAVE ANOTHER WEE IN A MINUTE.'

'I don't mind another, if you're offering,' said Niall. 'I have a fair thirst on me this morning.'

He was back to his usual cheerful self. In spite of having to downgrade his degree on his CV, he'd managed to secure a contract at the Castle Museum in York, starting early in the New Year. He planned to go home to Dublin for Christmas to see his mum, and then return to find cheap digs in York.

All in all, things had worked out pretty well.

Except for Grazyna. But Liz was still hopeful that might turn out okay in the end.

Grazyna had had to come clean about being in the country illegally. Her case was pending and wasn't likely to be heard until sometime in the spring. In the meantime, to Lukasz and Eryk's delight, she'd decided to stay in Whitby. Less to their delight, however, they'd also had to start school. They still had no idea about any of the immigration stuff, and probably wouldn't unless things didn't go Grazyna's way and she had no choice but to tell them. In the meantime, she was bearing it all in her usual, stoic way.

'You will have to move,' Grazyna said to Iris. 'I cannot reach the ceiling.'

'CAN'T YOU JUST PAINT AROUND ME?'

'No. Move, please.'

'LET ME FINISH MY TEA.'

'I thought you said you needed the toilet?'

'I DO, BUT IN MY OWN TIME. I'VE HAD A HEART ATTACK, YOU KNOW.'

'Angina,' corrected Kevin.

'IT FELT LIKE A HEART ATTACK.' Iris shuddered. 'IF YOU'D SEEN THE THINGS I SAW...'

'The goat, you mean?' said Niall with a grin.

Iris scowled.

It turned out that the creature Liz had seen on the steps, and that Iris had seen in Neptune Yard, had been nothing more sinister than a goat. True, it was an exceptionally big goat – a black Boer – that had escaped from the petting zoo at Pannet Park. The zoo staff had been trying to capture it on the quiet, because they hadn't wanted to be held responsible for all the damage it had done in the town – all the broken fences, ruined gardens, and poor Mike Howson's smashed fish crates. It had finally been caught when the headmaster of the local primary school had found it sleeping in the sand pit, and had managed to trap it there. The zoo's escapades finally came to light, and they were forced to pay for all the damage.

'I couldn't believe it when I saw the photo of it in the *Bugle*,' said Kevin. 'I didn't think goats got that big.'

But Iris remained unconvinced. 'I KNOW WHAT I SAW.' She sniffed. 'AND WHAT I HEARD.'

'What you *heard* was my boys,' said Grazyna. 'Eryk and Lukasz.'

'To be fair,' said Liz, 'they still haven't admitted the other howls, the ones I heard, and the ones at the Duke of York.'

'That is true,' said Grazyna. 'That couldn't have been them. They were in their beds.'

Niall and Tilly exchanged a furtive look, but not quite furtive enough. Liz and Benedict both saw it.

'What?' said Liz.

'Nothing,' said Niall. He made a show of examining his paintbrush.

Benedict frowned at him. 'Come on. You know something. Spit it out.'

Niall and Tilly exchanged another look. 'Do you want to tell them?' asked Tilly. 'Or shall I?'

Niall sighed, then grinned. 'It was me.'

'What?' said Kevin. 'The howling?'

Niall nodded. 'Apart from the first ones, obviously.'

'But why?' asked Liz. 'Just to scare people?'

'No!' Niall looked affronted.

'To help me sell more T-shirts,' said Tilly. 'We sold quite a few just after Iris heard the Barghest, but then sales started to fall off again, so we decided to give them another a little push.'

'It did the trick, right enough,' said Niall.

'We sold out,' said Tilly.

Benedict laughed. 'I might have known.'

Liz had to admit it was a clever sales ploy, even though it had scared the wits out of her.

'My poor boys got blamed for it,' said Grazyna stonily.

Tilly looked contrite. 'They didn't really get into trouble, though, did they? Not for that second lot of howling. We'd have come clean if they had.'

Iris had been listening to it all, wrapped in her plastic sheeting.

'What do you think?' Liz asked her.

The old lady shook her head, then delivered her pronouncement.

'I KNOW WHAT I SAW AND WHAT I HEARD... IT WAS NO GOAT. AND IT WASN'T KIDS OR THAT DAFT IRISHMAN FANNYING ABOUT... IT WAS THE BARGHEST. THE DOG OF DEATH!'

AUTHOR'S NOTE

Whitby is, of course, a real place – a jewel of a town nestled on the North Yorkshire coast, on the edge of the North York Moors National Park. It's a popular tourist destination, most famous for being the birthplace of Colonial explorer Captain Cook, and the inspiration for Bram Stoker's gothic master-piece, *Dracula*.

The town's Goth Weekends first began in 1994 and now take place twice a year, in the spring and autumn. They started as an alternative music festival attended by Goths only, but then, in the mid-2000s, the October weekend started to attract large numbers of non-Goths in Halloween, horror, historical, fantasy and sci-fi costume. It now attracts many alternative visitors, including Victorian vampires, rockers, punks and steampunks. They bring a much appreciated injection of fun, music, and money into the town. For dramatic purposes, I've combined the two weekends into a single week at Halloween, but otherwise I've tried to keep the details as accurate as possible. A charity football match is traditional, played between the local Whitby newspaper – the *Whitby Gazette* (not the *Bugle*) – and the visiting Goths.

You can find Whitby Goth Weekend on Twitter and Facebook. If you ever get the chance to visit in person, I can highly recommend it!

I've done my best to keep Whitby's geography – its street names and layout – as close to the real thing as possible. I may, however, have made a few mistakes, and I've also taken a couple of liberties that I hope you'll forgive.

The White Horse and Griffin Hotel, where Liz and Benedict go for their heart-to-heart, is real. So is the Whitby Lolly Shop and the Duke of York pub, where Niall works. All are popular with locals and tourists. The Captain Cook Memorial Museum and Pannet Park are well-known attractions, and, of course, Whitby Abbey and St Mary's Church continue to attract visitors from all over the world. I have tried to describe them as accurately as possible.

Kipper Cottage and Gull Cottage are based on the two cottages closest to Fortune's Smokehouse, on Henrietta Street.

Neptune Yard is my own invention, although it is based on the real-life Kiln Yard that can be found at the bottom of the abbey steps. Whitby is famous for its yards and 'ghauts' – the spaces and alleyways between tiers of houses that were built back-to-back into the cliffs of Whitby, to house fishing families. Today, more than eighty yards still exist out of an original one hundred in the town. They have the most evocative names – Dark Yard, Elbow Yard, Duck's Yard, Arguments Yard, Loggerheads Yard. I have to admit I was a bit disappointed to learn the latter two were named after families rather than states of mind. Frayed tempers must have been common in these tiny, overcrowded places, where dozens of families lived cheek-by-jowl. With each cottage filled to over-flowing with family and extended family, inhabitants would often take their meals and even their baths outside in the yard! Nowadays, a respectful exploration into some of these tiny yards can still offer a real insight into life in the eigh-teenth-century fishing community.

Like Neptune Yard, the Full Moon café and Howson's fish shop are my own inventions.

The Barghest, however, is real.

Or, at least, its legend is.

In the eighteenth century the word 'ghost' was pronounced 'guest' in many parts of the North, with the word 'bar' meaning 'of the town'. In Whitby, the Barghest is a mythical, monstrous black dog with huge teeth and claws, but various versions exist in different regions of the northeast. Some are shapeshifters, others rattle chains, but they are always an omen of death. At the imminent passing of a notable person, the Barghest may appear, followed by all the other dogs of the local area in a kind of funeral procession, heralding the person's death with howling and barking. If anyone was to get in the Barghest's way, it would strike out with its paw and leave a wound that never heals. The archaeological dig at the Roman signalling station at Goldsborough really did uncover the spooky tomb Niall describes – the remains of a man and a huge dog locked in eternal combat. Or is it an eternal embrace?

I hope you've enjoyed spending time in Whitby with Liz McLuckie, in this, the second book in the Kipper Cottage Mystery series. Perhaps you'll join her – and me – for the next one, *Death at the Feast*?

Until then, happy armchair sleuthing!

If you'd care to leave a review on Amazon they are enormously helpful in getting books discovered by new readers and I would be grateful for you thoughts.

ABOUT THE AUTHOR

Jan lives just outside Edinburgh with her husband, three kids, a one-eye whippet and a fat black pug. Born in a colliery village in the North East of England, she cut her literary teeth on the great storytellers of the 60's and 70's - Wilbur Smith, Frank Yerby, Mary Renault, and Sergeanne Golon. She began her writing career as an advertising copywriter, and has since had novels published by Random House and HarperCollins, and original audio series produced by Audible UK. She also writes for tv.

Jan enjoys psychological thrillers and crime fiction of all kinds, from the coziest of cozies to the blackest of noirs.

You can find Jan at www.kippercottagemysteries.co.uk

ALSO BY JAN DURHAM

Kipper Cottage Mysteries

Death at the Abbey (Book 1)

Death at Neptune Yard (Book 2)

Death at the Feast (Book 3)